Over the phone she'd come across as brusque and spinsterish, so he'd been expecting a plain woman. But Veronica was anything but plain. She was utterly gorgeous. Leonardo suspected that he would have difficulty keeping his hands off her.

Already he wanted to run his fingers through her hair, to pull her to him and kiss her until she forgot all about what her father was like. Leonardo knew he could make women forget all sorts of things, especially once he got them into bed. Make himself forget, too. Sex soothed the dissatisfied beast in him. That, and gazing out at this hypnotic and wonderfully relaxing view.

Leonardo turned to look out across the sea for a long moment. Soon, Laurence's villa—and this view—would be his. But until then he'd have to make do with other methods of relaxation.

He turned back to face Veronica with his most charming smile in place, the one that always made it oh-so-easy when he came across a woman he wanted. And he wanted this one. More, Leonardo conceded, than he had in a long time.

Secret Heirs of Billionaires

There are some things money can't buy...

Living life at lightning pace, these magnates are no strangers to stakes at their highest. It seems they've got it all... That is, until they find out that there's an unplanned item to add to their list of accomplishments!

Achieved:

1. Successful business empire.

2. Beautiful women in their bed.

3. *An heir to bear their name?*

Though every billionaire needs to leave his legacy in safe hands, discovering a secret heir shakes up the carefully orchestrated plan in more ways than one!

Uncover their secrets in:

The Secret Kept from the Greek by Susan Stephens

Carrying the Spaniard's Child by Jennie Lucas

Kidnapped for the Tycoon's Baby by Louise Fuller

The Greek's Secret Son by Julia James

Claiming His Hidden Heir by Carol Marinelli

The Secret the Italian Claims by Jennie Lucas

Wed for His Secret Heir by Chantelle Shaw

The Heir the Prince Secures by Jennie Lucas

Look out for more stories in the
Secret Heirs of Billionaires series coming soon!

Miranda Lee

THE ITALIAN'S
UNEXPECTED LOVE-CHILD

HARLEQUIN PRESENTS®

Recycling programs
for this product may
not exist in your area.

ISBN-13: 978-1-335-41973-6

The Italian's Unexpected Love-Child

First North American publication 2018

Copyright © 2018 by Miranda Lee

Printed in U.S.A.

Born and raised in the Australian bush, **Miranda Lee** was boarding school educated, and briefly pursued a career in classical music before moving to Sydney and embracing the world of computers. Happily married, with three daughters, she began writing when family commitments kept her at home. She likes to create stories that are believable, modern, fast-paced and sexy. Her interests include meaty sagas, doing word puzzles, gambling and going to the movies.

Books by Miranda Lee

Harlequin Presents

Master of Her Virtue
Contract with Consequences
The Man Every Woman Wants
Not a Marrying Man

Marrying a Tycoon

The Magnate's Tempestuous Marriage
The Tycoon's Outrageous Proposal
The Tycoon's Scandalous Proposition

Rich, Ruthless and Renowned

The Italian's Ruthless Seduction
The Billionaire's Ruthless Affair
The Playboy's Ruthless Pursuit

Visit the Author Profile page
at Harlequin.com for more titles.

To my daughter Veronica, who has read all my books, and said nice things about every single one.

PROLOGUE

LAURENCE SHOOK HIS head as he read the investigator's report for the second time. Frustration consumed him, along with dismay. He'd assumed his daughter would be married by now. Married with children. She was twenty-eight, after all. Twenty-eight and beautiful. Very beautiful.

His eyes moved over to the photo attached to the report, his heart filling with pride when he saw that his genes had produced a truly gorgeous creature. Gorgeous, but childless.

Such a waste!

Sighing, he returned to re-read the report.

Veronica had been engaged three years earlier to a doctor she'd met at the children's hospital she worked in. She was a physiotherapist and her fiancé an orthopaedic surgeon. Tragically, he'd been killed in a motorcycle accident two weeks before their wedding. After that, there was no evidence of her ever dating anyone again. She didn't even seem to have many friends. She'd become a loner, still living with her mother and not doing much of anything besides work, which she did from home now, rather than in hospitals.

Laurence understood grief. He'd been devastated

when his wife of forty years had died several years ago, not of the cancer—which they'd both expected would take her, given she'd carried a dangerous cancer gene—but of a stroke. He'd retreated into himself after that, retiring permanently to the holiday home they'd bought together on the Isle of Capri, never looking at another woman, never wanting to move on, as the saying went. But he'd been seventy-two at the time of her death, not in his twenties. His daughter was still young, for pity's sake.

But she wouldn't stay young for ever. Men could father children for a long time, but women had a biological clock ticking away in their bodies.

As a geneticist, Laurence knew all about human bodies and human genes. His in-depth knowledge on the subject was the reason behind his having donated his sperm to Veronica's mother in the first place. His gesture had been inspired more by hubris than caring, however. Male ego. He hadn't wanted to go to his grave without passing on his oh-so-brilliant genes.

Laurence shook his head from side to side, remorse filling his soul, as well as guilt. He should have contacted his daughter after Ruth died. Then he would have been there for her when her fiancé had been killed.

But it was too late now, he accepted wretchedly.

He was dying himself—ironically, of cancer. Liver cancer. Too late to do anything, really. His prognosis was not good. Advanced liver cancer was not very forgiving, though he only had himself to blame. After Ruth had died, he'd drunk far too much for far too long.

'I did knock,' a male voice intruded. 'But you didn't answer.'

Laurence looked up and smiled.

'Leonardo! How lovely to see you. What brings you home so soon after your last visit?'

'It's *Papa's* seventy-fifth birthday tomorrow,' Leonardo said as he walked along the terrace and sat down in the afternoon sunshine, sighing appreciatively as he gazed out at the sparkling blue Mediterranean. '*Dio*, Laurence. What a lucky man you are to have a view like this.'

Laurence glanced over at his visitor with admiring eyes. How well Leonardo looked. How handsome. And how full of life. Of course, Leonardo was only thirty-two, and a man of many talents—not least of which was everything women would find both fascinating and irresistible.

This last thought evoked a deep thoughtfulness.

'*Mamma* said she invited you to the party but you declined. It seems you have to go back to England tomorrow to see your doctor.'

'Yes, that's right,' Laurence agreed as he folded the report carefully so that Leonardo couldn't see it. 'My liver's playing up.'

'You do look a little jaundiced. Is it serious?'

Laurence shrugged. 'At my age, everything is serious. So, have you to come to play chess and listen to some decent music, or to try to buy my home again?'

Leonardo laughed. 'Can I do all three?'

'You can try. But my answer to selling this place will be no, as usual. When I'm dead and gone you can buy it.'

Leonardo looked startled, then uncharacteristically sombre. 'I hope that won't be for some years yet, my friend.'

'That's kind of you to say so. Now, do you want me

to open a bottle of wine or not?' he asked as he rose from his chair, carrying the report with him.

'Are you sure that's wise, under the circumstances?'

Laurence's smile was wry. 'I don't think a glass or two is going to make much difference at this stage.'

CHAPTER ONE

Veronica smiled as she accompanied her last client of the day to the front door. Duncan was eighty-four, and a darling, despite suffering terribly from sciatica. But he wasn't a complainer, which Veronica admired.

'Same time next week, Duncan?'

'Can't, love. Wish I could. You keep me going, you really do. But it's my granddaughter's twenty-first next week and I'm flying up to Brisbane for her party. Thought I might stay a week or two at my son's place while I'm there. Be warmer, for starters. This last winter in Sydney has got right into my bones. I'll give you a call when I get back.'

'Okay. Now, you have a good time, Duncan.'

She watched Duncan shuffle his way down Glebe Point Road in the direction of the small terraced house where he lived. Most of her clients were locals, elderly people with lots of aches and pains, though she did treat a smattering of students from nearby Sydney University. Young men, mostly, who played rugby and soccer and came to her for help with their various injuries.

Frankly, she preferred dealing with her older male clients. They didn't try to hit on her.

Not that she couldn't handle the occasional pass.

Veronica had been handling male passes since she'd reached puberty, the natural consequence of having been born good-looking. No point in pretending she wasn't. She'd been very blessed in the looks department, with a pretty face, dark, wavy hair, good skin and large violet eyes.

Jerome had called her a natural beauty.

Jerome...

Veronica closed her eyes for a few seconds as she tried to wipe all thought of that man from her mind. But it was impossible. Jerome's sudden death had been hard enough to handle, but it was what she'd learned after his death that had truly shattered her.

She still could not believe that he'd been so...so wicked.

Naive of her, she supposed, given what her mother had suffered at the hands of the man *she'd* married. Still, as she'd grown up, Veronica had never bought into her mother's cynicism towards the opposite sex. She'd always liked men. Liked and admired them. Yes, she'd grown up understanding that some men were players. But she'd always steered well clear of those. When a couple of her boyfriends had proved to be a bit loose on the moral side, neither of them had lasted long.

Veronica wasn't a prude. But she couldn't abide men who flouted society's rules just for the hell of it—who were disrespectful, insensitive or downright reckless. Her perfect man—the one she'd always envisaged marrying—would be none of those things. He'd be successful, and preferably handsome. But most importantly he would be decent and dependable. After all, he wasn't going to be just her husband. He was going to be the father of her children. At least four children, she'd always pictured. No single-child family for her.

When Jerome had come along, she'd thought he was perfect husband-and-father material.

But Jerome had not been perfect at all. Far from it.

Veronica gritted her teeth as she walked down the hallway towards the kitchen. She supposed she still had her work. Her personal life might be a non-event, with her dreams of a happy family shattered and her trust in relationships totally destroyed, but her professional life was still there. There was a lot of satisfaction in easing other people's pain.

Veronica was just filling the kettle with water when her mobile rang.

Probably someone wanting to make an appointment, she thought as she pulled her phone out of her pocket. She didn't get many personal calls these days.

'Yes?' she answered a little more abruptly than usual. Thinking about Jerome had left a residue of simmering anger.

'Is that Miss Veronica Hanson?' a male voice asked; a rich male voice with a slight accent. Possibly Italian.

'Yes, speaking,' she confirmed.

'My name is Leonardo Fabrizzi,' he said, at which point Veronica almost dropped her phone. Her fingers clutched it more tightly as she tried to get her head around who was on the other end of the line.

Because surely there couldn't be too many Italians called Leonardo Fabrizzi in this world?

It had to be him. Though perhaps not. The world was full of coincidences.

'Leonardo Fabrizzi, the famous skier?' she blurted out before she could think better of it.

There was dead silence for a few tense seconds.

'You *know* me?' he said at last.

'No, no,' she denied quickly, because of course she didn't *know* him. Though, she'd met him. Once. Several years ago, at an *après ski* party in Switzerland. They hadn't been properly introduced, so of course he would not recognise her name. But *he'd* been very famous at the time, a world-champion downhill racer with a reputation for recklessness, both on the slopes and off. His playboy status was well deserved, she'd learned that night, shuddering at how close she'd come to becoming just another of his passing conquests.

'I… I've heard of you,' she hedged, her voice still a little shaky. 'You're famous in the ski world and I like skiing.'

More than liked. She'd been obsessed with the sport for a long time, having been introduced to it as a teenager by a classmate's family. They'd been very wealthy and had taken her along on their skiing holidays as company for their very spoilt but not very popular daughter.

'I am no longer a famous skier,' he told her brusquely. 'I retired from that world some time ago. I am just a businessman now.'

'I see,' she said, not having skied herself since Jerome had died. Her interest in the sport—and most other things—had died along with the man she'd been going to marry.

'So how may I help you, Mr Fabrizzi?' It suddenly occurred to her that maybe he'd come here to Australia on business and was in urgent need of treatment after a long flight. He might have looked up Sydney physiotherapists online and come up with her website.

'I am sorry,' he said in sombre tones, 'But I have some sad news to tell you.'

'Sad news?' she echoed, startled and puzzled. 'What kind of sad news?'

'Laurence has died,' he told her.

'Laurence? Laurence who?' She knew no one called Laurence.

'Laurence Hargraves.'

Veronica was none the wiser. 'I'm sorry, but that name means nothing to me.'

'Are you *sure*?'

'Positive.'

'That is strange, because your name meant something to him. You're one of the beneficiaries in his will.'

'What?'

'Laurence left you something in his will. A villa, actually, on the Isle of Capri.'

'*What?* Oh, that's ridiculous! Is this some kind of cruel joke?'

'I assure you, Miss Hanson, this is no joke. I am the executor of Laurence's will, and have a copy of it right in front of me. If you are the Miss Veronica Hanson who lives in Glebe Point Road, Sydney, Australia, then you are now the proud owner of a very beautiful villa on Capri.'

'Goodness! This is incredible.'

'I agree,' he said, with a somewhat rueful note in his voice. 'I was a close friend of Laurence and he never mentioned you. Could he have been a long-lost relative of some kind? A great-uncle or a cousin, perhaps?'

'I suppose so. But I doubt it,' she added. Her mother was an only child and her father—even if he knew of her existence—certainly wouldn't have an English name like Hargraves in his family. He'd been an impoverished university student from Latvia who had sold his sperm for money and wasn't even on her birth certificate, which said *'father unknown'*. 'I'll have to ask my mother. She might know.'

'It is very puzzling, I admit,' the Italian said. 'Maybe Laurence was a patient of yours in the past, or a relative of a patient. Have you ever worked in England? Laurence used to live in England before he retired to Capri.'

'No, I haven't. Never.' She had, however, been to the Isle of Capri. For a day. As a tourist. Many years ago. She recalled looking up at the hundreds of huge villas dotted over the hillsides and thinking you would have to be very rich to live in one of them.

Veronica wondered if Leonardo Fabrizzi was still rich. And still a playboy.

Not that I care, shot back the tart thought.

'It is a mystery, all right,' the man himself said. 'But it doesn't change the fact that you can take possession of this property once the appropriate papers are signed and the taxes paid.'

'Taxes?'

'Inheritance taxes. I have to tell you that, on a property of this considerable value, the taxes will not come cheap. Since you are not a relative, they stand at eight percent of the current market value.'

'Which is what, exactly?'

'Laurence's villa should sell for somewhere between three-and-a-half and four million euros.'

'Heavens!' Veronica had a substantial amount of money in her savings account—she spent next to nothing these days—but she didn't have eight percent of four million euros.

'If that is a problem, then I could lend you the money. You could repay me when you sell.'

His gesture surprised her. 'You would do that? I mean…it could take some time to sell such a property, couldn't it?'

'Not in this circumstance. I would like to buy Laurence's villa myself. I often visited him there and I love the place.'

Veronica should have been grateful for such an easy solution. But for some reason she was reluctant just to say *yes, that would be great, yes, let's do that*.

He must have picked up on her hesitation, despite her not saying a word.

'If you're worried that I might try to cheat you,' he said, sounding somewhat peeved, 'you could get an independent valuation. Which amount I would be happy to pay in full. And in cash,' he added, highlighting just how rich he was.

Veronica rolled her eyes, never at her best when confronted by people who trumpeted their wealth. Jerome's parents had been very rich. And had never let her forget it, always saying she was a very lucky girl to be marrying their one and only child.

Hardly lucky, as it turned out.

'Perhaps you would like some time to think about all this,' the Italian went on. 'I imagine this has all come as a shock.'

'More of a surprise than a shock,' she said.

'But a pleasant one, surely?' he suggested smoothly. 'Since you didn't know Laurence personally, his death won't have upset you. And the sale of his villa will leave you very comfortably off.'

'Yes, I suppose so,' she mused aloud.

'I do hope you don't think me rude, Miss Hanson, but I noticed your birth date on the will. I know women don't like to talk about their ages but could you please confirm for me that the details are correct?' And he rattled off the date.

'Yes, that's correct,' she said, frowning. 'Though how this Laurence person knew it, I have no idea.'

'So you were twenty-eight as of last June.'

'Yes.'

'You're a Gemini.'

'Yes. Though I don't think I'm all that typical.' According to a book on star signs she'd once read, she could be light-hearted and fun-loving one day, and serious and thoughtful the next. That might have been true once but she seemed to be stuck these days on the serious and thoughtful. 'You believe in star signs, Mr Fabrizzi?'

'Of course not. It was just an idle remark. A man is master of his own destiny,' he stated firmly.

Spoken like a typically arrogant male, Veronica thought, but didn't say so.

'You're sure you know of no one called Laurence Hargraves?' he persisted.

'Absolutely sure. I have a very good memory.'

'It is all very curious,' the Italian admitted.

'True. I'm finding it pretty curious myself. So, do you mind if I ask *you* a few questions?'

'Not at all.'

'Firstly, how old was my benefactor?'

'Hmm. I'm not quite sure. Let me think. Late seventies, is my best guess. I know he was seventyish when his wife died, and that was some years back.'

'Quite elderly, then. And a widower. Did he have any children?'

'No.'

'Brothers and sisters?'

'No.'

'What did he die of?'

'Heart attack. Though I found out after the autopsy that he also had liver cancer. He told me the weekend before he died that he was going to London to see a doctor about his liver. Instead, all he did was make a will, then dropped dead shortly after leaving his solicitor's office.'

'Goodness.'

'Perhaps a mercy. The cancer was end stage.'

'Was he a heavy drinker?'

'I wouldn't have said excessively so. But who knows what a lonely man does in private?'

Veronica was taken aback at how sad he suddenly sounded. This evidence of empathy made her like Leonardo Fabrizzi a little bit, which was a minor miracle. Playboys were not her favourite species.

Though maybe she was doing him an injustice. Maybe he *had* changed. It was, after all, several years since the night he'd cast his charismatic eye on her and casually suggested she join him and the blonde dripping all over him for a threesome.

No, she thought with a derisive curl of her top lip, men like that didn't change. Once a player, always a player.

'If you give me your email address,' he continued, 'I'll send you a copy of the will and you can get back to me with your decision in a day or two. Alternatively, I could ring you at this time tomorrow and we can talk some more. Would that be suitable?'

'Not really.' She and her mother always went down

to the local Vietnamese restaurant for dinner early on a Saturday evening. 'What time is it in Italy at the moment?' she asked, not liking the idea of waiting to make a decision. 'You are in Italy, aren't you?'

'*Si*. I'm in Milan. In my office. It is nine-twenty.'

He really did speak beautiful English, very polished with correct grammar, all in a mild but disturbingly attractive accent. Veronica had always found Italian men attractive, having met quite a few during her obsessive skiing years.

One, however, stood out amongst all the rest…

'Right,' she said crisply. 'The thing is, I would like to talk to my mother first. Ask her if she ever knew a Laurence Hargraves. Maybe she can clear up this mystery for us. But, no matter what I find out, I can't see there will be any problem with your buying the villa, Mr Fabrizzi. Much as it would be lovely to have a holiday home on Capri, I really can't afford it. I will ring you back in about an hour or so. Okay?'

'*Certo*. I will look forward to your call, Miss Hanson.'

They exchanged relevant details, after which he hung up, leaving Veronica feeling slightly flustered. Which irritated the hell out of her. She thought she was over being affected by any member of the opposite sex, especially one with Leonardo Fabrizzi's dubious reputation.

Giving herself a mental shake, she retreated down the hallway and made her way up the stairs to the extension her mother had had built a few years back, a necessity once Nora had started up her home-help business on the Internet. The upstairs section included a small sitting room, a well-appointed office and a spacious bedroom and *en suite*. As it turned out, the extension had become a real blessing after Jerome's death, with Veronica able to convert her mother's old front bedroom into a treatment room for her own home-based physiotherapy business.

It wasn't until Veronica reached the upstairs landing that her thoughts returned to the annoyingly fascinating Italian and the astonishing reason behind his call. All of a sudden, an idea of who Laurence Hargraves might be zoomed into her head. An astonishing idea, really. Not very logical, either, knowing her mother. But the idea persisted, bringing with it a strange wave of alarm. Her heartbeat quickened and her stomach tightened, sending a burst of bile up into her throat. She swallowed convulsively, telling herself to get a grip.

What you are thinking is insane! Insane and illogical! The man was English, not Australian. Besides, Mum would not lie to me—not over something like this.

Finally, after scooping in several deep breaths, she lifted her hand to tap on her mother's office door, annoyed to see her hand was shaking. Her mouth went dry. And her heart started pounding again. Not quite a panic attack, but something close.

'Yes?' came her mother's impatient query.

It took an effort of will to turn the knob and go into the room.

'Mum,' she said on entering, pleased that her voice wasn't shaking as well.

Her mother didn't look up from where she was frowning at the computer screen.

'Yes?' she repeated distractedly.

Veronica walked over to perch on the corner of her mother's desk, gripping the edges with white knuckles. 'Mum, does the name Laurence Hargraves mean anything to you?'

Veronica had seen people go grey with pain in the course of her work; seen all the blood drain from their faces. But she'd never seen her mother go that particular colour.

Strangely enough, as she watched her mother's reaction, Veronica no longer felt panic. Just dismay. And the fiercest disappointment. Because now she knew the answer to the mystery, didn't she?

'He was my father, wasn't he?' she said bleakly, before her mother admitted to anything.

Nora groaned, then nodded. Sadly. Apologetically.

Veronica groaned as well, her face screwing up with distress, her hands balling into fists in defence of the flood of emotion which threatened to overwhelm her. Not since she'd discovered the awful truth about Jerome had she experienced such shock and anger. Funny how you could suspect something, but when you were actually faced with some awful truth your first reaction was still pained disbelief, quickly followed by outrage and anger.

'Why didn't you tell me the truth?' she threw at her mother in anguished tones. 'Why give me that cock-and-bull story about my father being some impoverished sperm donor from Latvia? Why not just tell me you had an affair with a married man?'

'But I didn't have an affair with Laurence!' her mother denied, her face flushing wildly. 'It wasn't like that. You don't understand,' she wailed, gripping her cheeks with both hands as tears filled her eyes.

For the first time in her life, Veronica felt no pity for her mother's tears.

'Then how was it, Mum?' she asked coldly. 'Make me understand, especially why you didn't tell me the truth about my father's identity.'

'I... I couldn't tell you. I gave Laurence my word.'

Veronica could not believe she was hearing this. She'd given her word to some adulterer? The mind boggled.

'Well, your precious Laurence is dead and gone now,' Veronica snapped. 'So I don't think your giving him your word matters any more. I dare say you'll also be surprised to hear that my errant father has left me something in his will,' she finished up caustically. 'I've just received a call from the executor. I'm now the owner of a villa on the Isle of Capri. Lucky me!'

Nora just stared at her daughter, grey eyes blinking madly.

'But...but what about his wife?'

'She's dead too,' Veronica said bluntly. 'Quite a few years ago, apparently.'

'Oh...'

'Yes. Oh.'

Her mother just sat there, stunned and speechless.

'I think, Mum,' Veronica bit out, her arms crossing angrily as she tried to contain her emotions, 'That it's time you told me the truth.'

CHAPTER TWO

LEONARDO EMAILED OFF a copy of the will then settled back down at his desk, trying to put his mind to studying the designs for next year's winter range. But his mind wouldn't cooperate. It remained firmly on the call he'd just made to Sydney, Australia.

Who in hell *was* Veronica Hanson? And why had Laurence never mentioned her?

A great-niece, perhaps? Leonardo speculated. Most people did like to leave their estates to relatives.

Though, if that were the case, why not leave her some money as well? Why just leave her the villa, then leave the rest of his considerable portfolio of cash, bonds and shares to cancer research?

It was a mystery all right.

Hopefully, Miss Hanson's mother would provide some pertinent information.

Glancing at his watch, Leonardo saw that less than ten minutes had passed since he'd hung up. He could hardly expect a call back this soon.

Unfortunately.

Leonardo's sigh was one of exasperation. He had no hope of concentrating on anything until he heard back from Miss Hanson. Patience had never been one of his virtues. But he had no alternative on this occasion but to wait.

Still, he didn't have to wait in here, at his desk, pretending to work. Jumping up, he decided to get himself some coffee, bypassing his PA's offer to get it for him with the excuse that he needed some air.

Leonardo needed some air a lot. He'd described himself as a businessman to Miss Hanson. But whilst Leonardo had quite enjoyed setting up his top-of-the-range sportswear company—and making a huge success of it—being *just* a businessman was not the way Leonardo ever saw himself. He was a sportsman, a man of action. A doer, not a pencil pusher. He actually hated offices and desks. Loathed meetings of any kind. And despised sitting for too long.

His spirits lifted once he was outside the building and into the fresh air. The sun was shining and a mild breeze was blowing. Milan in late August was glorious, though too busy, of course, the streets filled with tourists.

Leonardo breathed in deeply and headed for his favourite cafe, which was tucked away down a cobbled side street and never too crowded. There, his espresso was already waiting for him by the time he reached the counter, the female *barista* having spotted him as he strode into their establishment. He drank the strong black liquid down in one gulp, as was his habit. She smiled at him as he smacked his lips in appreciation, her big brown eyes flashing flirtatiously. She was a very attractive girl, with the kind of dark eyes and hair which Leonardo especially liked.

'*Grazie,*' he said, then placed the empty cup back on the counter, keeping his own smile very brief and not in any way flirtatious. Best not to encourage the girl. She might think he wanted more from her than good service.

There was a time in his younger years when he would have jumped into bed with her weeks ago. But he had more control over his hormones these days. And he was miles more careful, having narrowly escaped being trapped into marriage by a fortune-hunting female a few years back, shuddering whenever he thought of how close he'd come to being shackled for life to a girl he didn't love.

Leonardo shuddered anew as he strode from the cafe and headed back to his office.

Of course, he could have refused to marry the girl, even if she *had* been pregnant. Which it had turned out she wasn't. But Leonardo hadn't been brought up that way, having it drummed into him as a young man that, if he ever fathered a child, he'd better marry the mother *pronto*. Because if he didn't do the honourable thing then he wasn't ever to bother coming home again.

Such an outcome would have been untenable to Leonardo. His parents meant the world to him. So, yes, he would have married the girl. And loved his child. But his life would not have been the life he'd planned for himself, which was no marriage and children until he was ready to settle down. Which he certainly hadn't been back then.

Thank God his uncle had stepped in and demanded another pregnancy test by an independent doctor. Leonardo's relief at the news there was no baby had been a lesson well learned. After that he never believed a girl when she said she was on the pill. And he always used a condom. *Always!*

As an added precaution, he only dated women these

days who were less likely to be looking at him as a meal ticket for life. Women with careers of their own. Money of their own. And minds of their own.

On Leonardo's part, he had no intention of marrying until he met the love of his life. Which he hadn't so far. Strange, given all the clever and attractive girlfriends he'd had. But none had captured his heart. None had inspired the kind of wild passion he'd always imagined being truly in love would engender. Yes, sex with them was satisfying. But not mind-blowing. It never compared to the thrill of hurtling down a snowy mountain, knowing that he was going faster than any of his competitors.

Leonardo sighed. Ah, those were the days. Days which would never be repeated, his many falls and injuries having caught up with him by the time he'd turned twenty-five, forcing his retirement from the sport. Yes, he'd been a famous skier, as Miss Hanson had pointed out. But fame was fleeting and life moved on. Seven years had passed since then; seven successful but, perversely, frustrating years. He should have been satisfied with his life. Fabrizzi Sport, Snow & Ski was doing very well, with stores in all the major cities in Europe. He'd become a wealthy man in his own right, not just the spoiled only grandson of a billionaire.

But Leonardo wasn't satisfied. Sometimes he was consumed with the most awful emptiness, the result perhaps of not having been able to fulfil his ambitions on the ski slopes, injury always having got in the way of success in major championships. There was a restlessness living inside him, a manic energy at times which refused to be quelled, no matter what he did.

And he did plenty. He still skied in the winter, though

not competitively. He went yachting and waterskiing in the summer, along with mountain climbing and abseiling. Recently, he'd gained his pilot's licence for both small planes and helicopters. His frequent holidays were hectic with activity, but he inevitably returned to work still burning with a fire undimmed.

The only time Leonardo had really relaxed was when he'd been on Capri, sitting on Laurence's terrace, looking out at the sparkling blue sea and sipping one of his friend's excellent wines.

Thinking of Capri sent his mind back to Laurence's mystery heiress. Hopefully she would ring him soon and tell him that he could buy the villa. Because he not only wanted it, he *needed* it. Life without Laurence's company would be bad enough. Life without the calming influence of his friend's beautiful home would be a bitter disappointment.

Leonardo glanced at his Rolex once more, then headed back to his office, not wanting to take Miss Hanson's call in the street.

CHAPTER THREE

VERONICA LAY ON her bed, her head whirling with what she'd discovered. She found it almost impossible to process her feelings. Was she still angry or just terribly sad? What her mother had told her had sort of made sense, and was much better than her mother having slept with a married man. And, yes, she understood why her mother had promised to keep her father's identity a secret, even if it still upset her.

What puzzled her the most, however, was the will. Now, that *didn't* make sense. Why leave her anything at all? Her father must have known it would stir up trouble and leave so many questions unanswered.

Her father...

Tears filled Veronica's eyes. She'd had a father. A real father, not some unnamed sperm donor. He hadn't been a nobody, either. He'd been a famous scientist, a groundbreaking geneticist with a brilliant brain. Oh, how she wished her mother had told her years ago.

But of course she hadn't been able to. She'd given her word. Down deep, Veronica understood that. Good people honoured their promises. And her mother was a good woman. But, dear God, her father was dead now.

Dead and gone. She could never see him or talk to him. Never know what he was like.

'Are you all right, love?' her mother asked tentatively from the doorway.

Veronica blinked away her tears then turned her head to smile softly at her very stressed-looking mother. She was well aware that her mother had suffered a big shock too. She had to be worried that her much-loved daughter might never forgive her.

Whilst Veronica still harboured some natural resentment at the situation, she could not blame her mother for what she'd done. If anyone was to blame, it was Laurence Hargraves. The stupid man should have gone to his grave with his secret intact and not left her anything at all! Then she could have gone on being blissfully unaware of having a father whom she would now never have the opportunity to know.

'I'll be fine,' she said with feigned composure. 'It's just a shock, that's all.'

'I know. And I'm so sorry. I don't know what possessed Laurence to put you in his will. I truly don't. It was sweet of him, in a way, but he must have known that the truth would come out, and that then you'd be upset.'

'People do strange things when they're dying,' Veronica said with a degree of understanding. She'd seen it time and time again in her work. Once, when she'd been treating an old lady, the woman had confessed she was dying and on impulse had wanted to give Veronica a beautiful ring she was wearing. Veronica had declined, knowing that the woman had a daughter who would have been most hurt by such a gesture. But the old lady hadn't thought of that. Maybe this Laurence hadn't thought through the consequences of his will.

Or maybe he'd known *exactly* what he doing.

The trouble was she would never really know either way. Because she didn't *know* the man.

'Would you like me to make you some coffee, love?' her mother asked.

'Yes, that would be nice,' she replied politely, thinking what she really wanted was to be left alone. She needed to think.

Her mother disappeared, leaving Veronica to ponder the reason why her father had chosen to make his identity known at this late stage, when he could no longer be a living presence in her life. What she wouldn't have given to have a real father when she'd been growing up, when she'd been at school, when her bitchy so-called *friends* would tease her about having come out of a test tube. She'd laughed at the time. But she hadn't found their jibes funny at all. The hurt had struck deep. Teenage girls, she'd found, had a very mean streak. It was no wonder she'd always gravitated to boys when making close friends.

Thinking of boys reminded Veronica that there was one very grown-up boy she would have to ring back shortly.

Leonardo Fabrizzi.

She wasn't looking forward to telling him that Laurence Hargraves was her biological father. He was sure to ask her lots of questions.

Still, she had lots of questions she wanted to ask him. After all, if he was close enough to her father to have been made executor of his will, then he had to have known him very well. Maybe he had a photo or two that he could send her. She would dearly love to know what this Laurence looked like.

Veronica was nothing like her mother in looks. Nora Hanson was quite short with brown hair, grey eyes and a rather forgettable face and figure. In truth, she was on the plain side. Veronica had always assumed she'd inherited her striking looks from her biological father. Maybe now she'd have the opportunity to see the evidence for herself.

This last thought propelled an idea into Veronica's brain which had her sitting up abruptly then scrambling off the bed. She raced out into the hallway and bolted down to the kitchen, where she snatched up her phone which she'd left lying on the counter.

'Goodness!' her mother said, startled perhaps by her sudden exuberance. 'Who are you ringing?'

'The Italian I told you about. Leonardo Fabrizzi. I promised to ring him back once I'd talked to you.'

'Oh,' Nora said, looking pained. 'You're not going to tell him everything, are you? I mean, does he have to know about your being Laurence's daughter? Can't you just sell him the villa and leave it at that?'

'No, Mum,' Veronica said firmly. 'I can't just leave it at that. And I *am* going to tell him I'm Laurence's daughter. For one thing, it makes a difference to the inheritances taxes if I'm a relative. On top of that, I won't be selling Mr Fabrizzi the villa straight away. There's something else I have to do first.'

'What?'

Veronica told her.

CHAPTER FOUR

LEONARDO'S HEART JUMPED when his phone finally rang, then began to race when he saw it was her at last. Why was he suddenly nervous? He wasn't a nervous person. On the ski slopes, he'd been known for his *nerve*, not his nervousness. The press had called him Leo the Lion because of his lack of fear. When he'd retired, he'd chosen the image of a lion as the logo for his sportswear company.

'Thank you for calling me back, Miss Hanson,' he answered, putting the phone on speaker as he leant back in his leather chair and did his best to act cool and businesslike. 'Was your mother able to tell you anything enlightening?'

'She certainly did.' Her answer was crisp, her voice possibly even more businesslike than his own. 'It seems that Laurence Hargraves was my biological father.'

Leonardo snapped forward on his chair. '*Mio Dio!* How did that happen?'

'It seems Mr Hargraves came to Australia about thirty years ago to do genetic research at the Sydney University. He was given a house as part of the deal and my mother was hired as his housekeeper.'

'And what? They had an *affair*?' Leonardo found the

concept of Laurence being unfaithful hard to believe. Laurence had been devoted to his wife. They'd been an inseparable couple, their love for each other very obvious to everyone who knew them.

'No, no, nothing like that. Though my mother said that she and Laurence became quite good friends during the two years she worked for him. With Ruth too. She said she was a lovely lady. No, they didn't have an affair, or even a one-night stand.'

'I don't understand, then.'

'Mum had me through IVF. I thought my biological father was an impoverished law student from Latvia who sold his sperm for money. That's what I'd always been told. But it was a lie. Laurence was the sperm donor.'

'I see… Well, that explains everything, I suppose. Though not the secrecy.'

'Did you know that Laurence's wife couldn't have children?'

'Not exactly. Though I did know they'd never had children. I didn't know which of them was the cause of their childlessness. Or whether they'd just decided not to have children. It's not something you can ask without being rude. Obviously, the problem was Ruth's.'

'Yes. Mum told me Ruth had very bad cancer genes which ran through her family and had killed off all her relatives. She decided as a young woman not to pass any of those genes on and had a total hysterectomy. She met Laurence through his work on genes and they fell in love. He told my mother he didn't overly mind about not having children as his love for Ruth was all-consuming. And so was his work. In fact, his work was the reason behind his becoming my biological father.'

'His *work* was the reason?' Leonardo was not quite getting the picture.

'Yes. When my mother confided to Laurence that she planned to have a baby through IVF at this particular clinic, he was appalled.'

'Appalled? Why?'

'Because he thought they didn't know enough about the prospective sperm donor's genes. Yes, the clinic records showed the one she'd chosen was tall, dark and handsome. *And* intelligent. But Laurence questioned his medical and mental backgrounds, the details of which he said were superficial at best. He said she was taking a risk because she didn't know enough about the sperm donor's DNA, whereas his own had been thoroughly checked out. By *him.*'

Leonardo nodded. Now he understood what had happened.

'So he offered his own sperm instead,' he said.

'Yes. When Mum initially refused, he argued with her about it. Made her feel that if she didn't agree she was being silly.'

Leonardo nodded. 'Laurence could be very persuasive when he wanted to be. He introduced me to classical music. And opera. I told him I hated opera but he proved me wrong in the end. Now I love it. I can well understand how he talked your mother into using his sperm. He would have convinced her that she owed it to her child to make sure she wasn't carrying any unfortunate genes. But what about Ruth? I gather she didn't know anything about this arrangement?'

'No. He insisted they keep it a secret from his wife. He said it would upset Ruth terribly if she found out. Mum had to promise to put "father unknown" on the birth certificate and go along with the charade of my father being a Latvian university student.'

'That makes Laurence sound a bit heartless.'

'That's what I thought. Mum said he wasn't but I don't agree. Okay, so he bought her the house we live in. Big deal! She still had to live on the single mother's pension until I went to school and she could go back to work. I mean… Okay, so he didn't want to upset his childless wife… I get that, I guess. But why didn't he contact Mum and me after his wife died? Why leave me to find out he was my father after he was dead? What good was that?'

'I'm sorry, I cannot answer those questions, Miss Hanson. I am as baffled as you are. But at least he left you his villa.'

'Yes. I've been thinking about that too. Why leave me anything at all? And why this villa? On the island of Capri, of all places. He must have had a reason. He was a highly intelligent man, from the sounds of things.'

Something teased at the back of Leonardo's mind. Something about the last day he'd talked to Laurence. But the thought didn't stick. He would think about it some more later, when he was calmer.

'Maybe he just wanted to give you something of value,' he suggested.

'Then why not just give me money? From reading his will, I gather he had plenty.'

'I must admit that thought had occurred to me too, Miss Hanson.'

'Oh, please stop calling me that. My name is Veronica.'

'Very well. Veronica,' he said, and found himself smiling for some reason. 'And you must call me Leonardo. Or Leo, if you prefer. I know Australians like to shorten names.'

'I prefer Leonardo,' she said. 'It sounds more… Italian.'

Leonardo laughed. 'I am Italian.'

'You speak beautiful English.'

'*Grazie.*'

'And *grazie* to you too. Now… I have made a decision about the villa. I appreciate your offer to buy it, Leonardo. And I will sell you the villa. *Eventually.* But, first, I want to come and stay there for a while. Not too long. Just long enough to find out all I can about my father…'

CHAPTER FIVE

EXCITEMENT FIZZED IN Veronica's stomach as the ferry left Sorrento on its twenty-minute ride to Capri. The day was glorious, not a cloud in the sky, the water a sparkling and very inviting blue.

It had taken two weeks for her to organise this trip. She hadn't wanted to leave her patients in the lurch by departing abruptly so she'd seen them all one more time—or contacted them by phone—telling them that she was taking a much-needed holiday.

Naturally, she hadn't been about to blurt out the truth behind her trip to Italy. That would have set a cat among the pigeons, sparking far too many questions. They'd all been sweetly understanding, bringing her to tears on a couple of occasions, because they mistakenly thought she was still grieving Jerome's death.

Which she had been, in a way. For far too long.

But not any more.

Finding out about her real father had been a big shock. But it had also given her the impetus to stop living her life like some mourning widow. Hence her new and rather colourful wardrobe, which had put a serious dent in her savings. But how could she come to this gorgeous and glamorous island looking drab and dreary?

Veronica refused to concede that the effort she'd made with her appearance had anything to do with Leonardo Fabrizzi. As nice as he'd been to her on the phone, he still was what he'd always been. A player.

Curiosity had sent Veronica looking him up on various social media sites and there'd been plenty to look at. Since his retirement from competitive downhill racing, Leonardo had made a name for himself in the world of fashion, Fabrizzi being considered *the* name in active wear. His company had boutiques in all the main cities in Europe, as well as one in New York. Veronica noted that the press articles didn't call them shops or stores. No. *Boutiques* they were called, the kind where only the rich and famous could afford to shop.

Aside from news about his business acumen, it showed Leonardo had also led a very active social life, his name connected with many beautiful women of the type wealthy playboys invariably attracted. Models. Actresses. Heiresses. He'd had countless gorgeous creatures on his arm over the years—and undoubtedly in his bed. Leopards didn't change their spots. And neither had Leo the Lion.

It was feminine pride, Veronica told herself, which had made her put her best foot forward today. And her best face. All women liked to feel attractive, especially when in the company of a man as handsome and as charismatic as Leonardo Fabrizzi.

And she would be in his company within the next half an hour. Leonardo had made all the arrangements with Veronica over the phone. He was going to meet her at the dock then take her straight to the villa which, she'd learned, was perched above the Hotel Fabrizzi, a small establishment which Leonardo's parents had been running for over a decade.

This news had surprised Veronica as she'd learned via the Internet that the Fabrizzis were from Milan, Leonardo's grandfather having set up a textile manufacturing company after the war, becoming extremely wealthy over the years. He'd had two sons and heirs, Stephano and Alberto. What she hadn't learned— though admittedly she hadn't looked very hard—was what had happened after the grandfather had died. After all, she was coming to Capri to find out about her own father's history, not Leonardo's.

Thinking once more of the reason behind this trip made her heart beat faster. Soon, hopefully, she'd have answers to all the questions this unexpected inheritance had raised. Soon, she'd find out everything she wanted to know about her biological father. What he'd looked like. What he'd liked. What he'd been *like*!

Veronica no longer harboured any lingering anger over her mother's lies. What was done was done. No point in going on and on about it. The blame—if there was any blame—lay at her father's feet. Okay, so she was still upset at his not having contacted her earlier. After all, if he had wanted to keep his identity a secret, why leave her his home in his will?

This was the question which bothered her the most. His leaving her this villa.

Why, Dad? Why?

Her heart caught at finding herself calling him Dad like that. Caught, then turned over. She'd never called the student from Latvia *Dad*, not even in her thoughts. He'd just been the sperm donor. Not a real person. Just some tadpoles in a test tube. She'd never tried to picture what he looked like. She'd blanked her mind to him. Not so Laurence Hargraves. He was real in her head. Very real. She couldn't stop thinking about him.

Tears pricked at her eyes, filling them quickly then threatening to spill over. When the girl seated across from her on the ferry started staring at her, Veronica found a smile from somewhere, blinking the tears away before pulling her phone from her straw bag. She'd promised her mum she would take photos of everything and send them to her.

So she did, starting with the ferry, the sea and the approaching island.

Leonardo wasn't on the pier waiting for her. Instead there was a middle-aged man holding a sign with her name on it. He looked very Italian, with curly black hair and dark eyes. Clearly, he didn't know what Veronica looked like, as he was scouring the crowd of tourists with a worried look on his face.

When she walked right up to him and introduced herself, his face broke into a radiant smile.

'Signora Hanson,' he said with a thick Italian accent, dark eyes dancing. 'Why, you are *molto bella*! Leonardo should have told me.'

Veronica smiled. She didn't speak Italian but she could recognise a compliment when she heard one.

'Where is Leonardo?' she asked, disappointed at his no-show.

'He said to tell you he is sorry. He was held up. Business. He is flying in soon.'

'*Flying* in? But there is no airport on Capri.'

'There is a helipad. At Anacapri. I am to give you a sightseeing tour then take you there to meet him. Here.

Let me take your luggage.' He tossed the sign with her name on it in a nearby bin.

Veronica didn't have the heart to tell him she didn't really want a sightseeing tour, so she just smiled and said, 'How lovely,' then climbed into the back of a long yellow convertible that looked like a relic from an early Elvis Presley film.

She was glad after less than a minute that she'd put her hair back into a secure ponytail. The breeze coming off the sea—plus the wind caused by Franco's rather cavalier driving—would not have made for a pretty result. Veronica tried to appreciate the sights but she really wasn't in the mood. She'd been so looking forward to meeting Leonardo her disappointment was acute. She politely declined a visit to the Blue Grotto, admitting at that stage that she had been to Capri once before, many years ago, her one-day tour having included a visit to the grotto.

'It's a lot busier these days,' she said, noting the long line of boats waiting to go into the famous cave.

Franco frowned. '*Too* busy. But, come the end of September, things will be better. The cruise ships. They will stop coming. Will you be here then?'

'Unfortunately not.' September had only just arrived and her return flight was for just over three weeks' time.

'It is too warm for the top to be down,' Franco decided at this point, and pressed a button which sent a canvas top up and over, shading her from the sun. Which was perhaps just as well, Veronica's pink-and-white striped top having a deep boat neckline which might catch the sun on her neck. She always lathered herself in sunscreen. She didn't want to burn.

Once Veronica put aside her disappointment over

Leonardo's no-show, she enjoyed the tour. Franco was a very agreeable guide, his knowledge of the island that of a man born and bred there. It turned out he was also married to Leonardo's older sister, Elena. They had three children, a boy and two girls.

She wondered if Leonardo had told him she was Laurence's daughter. Possibly not yet, she decided, swallowing back the questions she was dying to ask about her father. Maybe another day…

Finally, after getting a text on his phone, Franco headed for Anacapri and the helipad.

Despite telling herself there was nothing to be nervous about, Veronica's stomach tightened and her heartbeat quickened. By the time Franco reached the top of the hill and parked, she found she could not sit in the back of the taxi any longer. Leaving her straw carryall on the back seat, she climbed out and walked around, lecturing herself all the while about her upcoming meeting with Leonardo.

Yes, he's very attractive, but he's a playboy, Veronica. Quite a notorious one. Don't ever forget that. Play it cool when you come face to face with him. Don't, for pity's sake, let his good looks—and his undoubted charm—distract you from your quest. You've come here to find out about your father, not flutter your eyelashes at Leonardo Fabrizzi.

A helicopter approached from the direction of the mainland. Veronica shaded her eyes to watch it, despite already wearing sunglasses. The helicopter was black with red writing on the side and tinted glass, so she couldn't see who was sitting in it. As it came in to land, the wind from the huge rotor blades hit her like a mini tornado. Thank God she'd chosen to wear her new white jeans, and not the sundress with its gathered skirt. As it was, a few strands of hair came loose from her ponytail, whipping across her face. Finally, the helicopter's noisy engine shut down and the blades slowed. A side door on it slid open and out jumped a man, a tall dark-haired man in a pale grey suit and a blinding white shirt open at the neck with no tie.

Veronica recognised Leonardo instantly, despite his hair—which he'd worn disgracefully long back in his skiing days—now being cropped short. It suited him, however, showing off his face to better advantage, highlighting his sculptured features and strong jawline. Still, she'd already known about his new haircut, having studied many images on social media during the last two weeks.

He was, however, even better looking in the flesh than in recent photos, two-dimensional images not able to capture the total essence of this man. He was, Veronica accepted as she watched him stride towards her, not just the stereotype of tall, dark and handsome. Leonardo was more than that. Much more, as evidenced by the way her heart began racing within her chest. Aside from his looks, there was the way he moved. The way he walked. The set of his broad shoulders. The angle of his head. He was the total male package. Arrogant. Confident. And super sexy.

As he drew nearer, her heartbeat accelerated further.

Did he do this to all women? she wondered with exasperation. Did he make them forget everything that life had taught them about males of the 'player' species? Did he make them want to act like fatuous female fools?

Possibly.

Probably!

Veronica sarcastically renamed him 'tall, dark and dangerous' in her head.

It was a good thought to have. A sensible, soothing thought, giving her the willpower to draw in several deep, gathering breaths, consciously slowing her heart-beat and untangling the knots in her stomach. No way was she going to have her head turned by Leonardo Fabrizzi. She'd avoided that trap all those years ago. Surely she was better equipped not to fall for it this time.

All you have to do is think of Jerome...

He was staring at her, she knew, despite his sun-glasses hiding the expression in his eyes. She could sense his penetrating gaze behind the opaque lenses, perhaps because his dark brows were drawn slightly to-gether, forming two little frowning lines. It made her glad she was wearing sunglasses herself. That way he wouldn't see into her eyes which she knew were, in-deed, the windows to her soul.

Not that her *soul* was bothered by Leonardo Fab-rizzi. It was her body which was bothered currently. Her silly, possibly frustrated female body which had been too long without the comfort of a man's arms around her, without the wonderful feeling of being held, kissed and caressed.

'Veronica?' he said in that sexy voice which by now she was familiar with.

Her smile felt forced. 'Yes,' she confirmed.

His smile was light. And wry. 'I should have known you'd be beautiful,' he said. 'Laurence was a very hand-some man. Welcome to Capri,' he added, stepping for-ward to draw her into a very Italian hug.

Her arms were trapped by her side as he pulled her close, the strength and warmth of his body bypassing her resolve to be sensible around him. *Oh, God.* She could feel herself melting in his arms. Feel her blood charge hot and heady around her veins. Her neck flushed. So did her face.

'Goodness!' she exclaimed, pulling back out of his embrace before she combusted. 'I'd forgotten how very demonstrative Italians were.'

Leonardo's eyebrows arched. 'You don't hug hello in Australia?'

'We do. Though usually just relatives and close friends.'

'How very odd. If I overstepped the mark, then I apologise. Come. It is too hot to be standing out here in the sun.' He took her elbow and turned her back towards where the taxi waited for them, Franco still behind the wheel.

She resisted pulling her arm away, thinking that would be too rude. And too telling. He was just being a gentleman, after all. But, oh, it worried her, that wildly pleasurable sensation which had charged up her arm at his touch.

'You don't have any luggage?' she asked when he dropped her arm to open the back door of the taxi.

'No need. I keep spare clothes here at my parents' hotel. My Capri clothes, I call them. No business suits for me when I stay here, isn't that so, Franco?' he said as he handed her into the car and climbed in after her.

'*Si*, Leo. You are a different man once you come here.'

'Have you been looking after our visitor? Shown her the more famous sights?'

'*Si*. But Veronica, she not want to go to Blue Grotto.'

'I've seen it before.' Veronica jumped in before Franco could say anything further. 'I came here as a day tripper when I was in my early twenties. It's a very beautiful cave but I didn't want to queue up to see it again.'

Leonardo nodded. 'Understandable. Actually, the only way to see Capri is by air. I will take you up in the helicopter tomorrow.'

'Oh,' she said, thrilled and terrified by his offer. 'You don't have to do that.'

'But I want to. And you will love it. Let's go, Franco. I'm sure Veronica is anxious to see her father's villa.'

Oh, Lord, Veronica thought as the taxi moved off. Her father's villa. The reason she'd come here. And the last thing she'd been thinking about since the very handsome Leonardo Fabrizzi had stepped off that helicopter less than five minutes ago.

CHAPTER SIX

LEONARDO SETTLED INTO the back seat of the taxi and tried to act normally, not like a man who was finding the girl next to him disturbingly attractive. Disturbing, because he wasn't in the mood to be attracted to *any* girl at the moment, having decided after today's fiasco in Rome that the female sex was nothing but trouble.

At the same time, he owed it to his friend's memory to be hospitable to his daughter. And to satisfy Veronica's very natural curiosity about the father she'd never known. It was a pity, however, that she had to possess the type of allure which he'd always found difficult to resist. He adored tall, elegantly slender brunettes, especially one whose hair was long and which, once released from a ponytail prison, would cascade down her back in loose curls like the tresses of some mediaeval princess. Combine that with a delicate oval face, clear porcelain skin and a lush mouth and you had a package which would tempt a saint.

And he was no saint.

Hopefully, when she took her sunglasses off, she would have small squinty eyes and a bumpy nose, but he doubted it. Laurence's eyes had been one of his best features and his nose had been nicely shaped. If his daughter took after him—and he suspected that she did—she would be a classical beauty, with a superb brain and an enquiring mind.

The many hours Leonardo had spent with Laurence stood out as some of the most enjoyable times of his adult life. It hadn't been just his house he'd enjoyed but the man himself. His company. His knowledge. His probing questions.

Leonardo sighed as he was reminded how much he missed his friend.

'I'm sorry I wasn't there to meet you off the ferry, Veronica,' he said. 'I had some unexpected trouble at my boutique in Rome which I had to attend to.'

She turned to glance his way, her jeaned thigh briefly brushing against his. 'Something serious?'

'Yes and no. The manager was…what is the expression?…dipping her fingers in the till.'

'That's dreadful. Did you have her arrested?'

Leonardo's laugh was very dry. 'I would have liked to, but she threatened to ruin me if I did that.'

'How could she ruin you?'

Leonardo shrugged. 'Perhaps "ruin" is an exaggeration. She threatened to accuse me of sexual harassment if I had her arrested. In the end, I paid her off and she left quietly. But I'm not sure I trust her to keep her silence. She might still put something nasty on social media about me.'

'Like what?'

'She could say that to get her job in the first place she had to sleep with me.'

'But that's slander!'

'Not exactly. I did sleep with her. Once. It was a

mistake, but I could not take it back after it happened, could I?'

'Well, no. I guess not.'

Leonardo noted the dry note in Veronica's voice. She probably thought he was a playboy. Which he was, in some people's eyes. But not of the worst kind. He tried not to hurt women's feelings, but unfortunately the opposite sex often equated lust with love. He glanced over at Veronica and wondered if she was that type.

This thought brought another one.

'I didn't think to ask over the phone if you had a boyfriend,' he said. They'd talked about their professional lives but hadn't touched on the personal. He'd told her about his sportswear company and she'd explained that she worked from home as a physiotherapist, treating mostly elderly patients. She'd sounded oddly spinsterish over the phone. He could see now how wrong that impression had been. A beautiful woman like her would surely have a love life.

Her face betrayed nothing. But she stiffened a little.

'No,' she replied after a small hesitation. 'No one at the moment. No one serious, at least,' she added with a wry little smile.

'Ah. You like to play the field.'

Her laugh was both light and amused. 'If you like...'

He did like. Oh, yes, he liked that idea a lot, forgetting all about the antagonism towards the opposite sex that this morning's confrontation had evoked in him. Suddenly, the prospect of keeping this lovely lady company this coming weekend was not a duty but a pleasure.

'We have arrived,' he announced when Franco

turned his taxi through the high stone walls into the courtyard of the Hotel Fabrizzi. 'What do you think, Veronica? Is not my parents' hotel a delightful little establishment?'

CHAPTER SEVEN

HARDLY *LITTLE*, VERONICA THOUGHT, glad to turn her eyes away from this extremely handsome and annoyingly charismatic man. Lord, but he could charm the pants off any woman!

Except me, she reassured herself, blithely ignoring her thudding heartbeat.

'It's lovely,' she said as the taxi came to a halt in front of a columned portico.

The hotel itself was two-storeyed and dazzlingly white, with terracotta tiles on the roof and dark wooden frames around the windows and doors. To their right as they alighted was a large pergola covered in grape vines, under which sat a long wooden table with equally long benches on either side and two large cushioned chairs at each head of the table. The closest was occupied by a huge ginger cat, basking in the dappled sunshine. When Leonardo walked over to stroke it, it purred loudly but did not get up.

'This is Gepetto. He's my mother's cat and very old. He was here when my parents bought this place thirteen years ago. The previous owners abandoned him.' Leonardo smiled a rueful smile. 'He's not de-sexed. Mostly because we can never get him into a cage. He doesn't mind being stroked but don't ever try to pick him up. He can be quite savage. I'm told there are many ginger kittens on Capri.'

Veronica looked at Leonardo and wondered how many offspring *he'd* sired over the years. Though perhaps he was too careful for that. Wealthy playboys would learn to practise safe sex from an early age, she imagined. There certainly hadn't been anything about paternity suits levelled against him on the Internet.

'Must go, Leo,' Franco called out as he dropped Veronica's case onto the portico then climbed back into the taxi. 'I will see you tonight,' he directed straight at her.

'Tonight?' Veronica echoed but Franco was already gone.

'My parents will invite you to dinner,' Leonardo explained. 'The whole family will be there to meet you. They are very curious over the long-lost daughter of their friend and neighbour.'

'Oh.' It sounded like there would be a daunting lot of people gawking at her.

'Don't say no,' he advised. 'They would be most offended if you did.'

'I wouldn't dream of saying no,' she said, just as two people emerged from the hotel out into the sunny courtyard.

Veronica saw immediately where Leonardo got his looks, because this had to be his parents. Both of them were surprisingly tall for Italians. Despite being obviously in their seventies, they both stood with straight backs, their faces beaming with happiness at the sight of their son.

'Leonardo!' his mother exclaimed, and hurried over to throw her arms around him.

'*Mamma*,' he said warmly, holding his mother's face and covering it with kisses.

His mother laughed and smiled, hugging him even tighter.

Veronica watched with a tightness in her own chest. Was it jealousy she was feeling? Or just envy? She and her mother loved each other dearly but they weren't much into physical demonstrations of their love. The occasional hug, maybe. Her mother had kissed her good-bye at the airport. Just one kiss. On the cheek.

Of course, Italians were like this. They were a passionate people, given to touching and kissing at the drop of a hat. Australians not so much, though they were improving when it came to showing affection—especially in Sydney, where immigration was the highest, with people from other cultures bringing with them new and possibly better ways.

Finally, Signora Fabrizzi disentangled herself from her son's arms and turned to face Veronica whilst Leonardo's father had his turn at hugging and kissing his son.

'And you must be Veronica,' she said, her Italian accent not as heavy as Franco's. 'Laurence's secret daughter. I am Sophia, Leonardo's *mamma*. And this is Alberto, his *papa*. My, but you are lovely, aren't you? Let me see your eyes,' she added, and without a by-your-leave stepped forward and swept off Veronica's sunglasses.

'*Mamma!*' Leonardo chided, but laughing. 'Don't be rude.'

'I just wanted to see if she had Laurence's eyes,' his mother explained sheepishly. 'See, Leonardo? They are the same violet colour. The same shape. Now I believe she is really his daughter.'

Leonardo muttered something in Italian, having removed his own sunglasses, perhaps so that he could see the colour of Veronica's eyes more clearly. Their eyes met, with nothing now to mask their feelings. Veronica stiffened at the naked desire which zoomed across the space between them. It was the same way he'd looked at her that night all those years ago. She'd resisted him then. But could she resist him now? Did she even *want* to?

Hopefully, he wouldn't put that question to the test. Because, for whatever reason, she didn't feel as strong today as she had back then. Which was odd, really, since she had her experience with Jerome to help immunise her against the attractions of men such as Leonardo Fabrizzi. She wished now that she hadn't suggested she was the free and easy type when it came to men. The urge to seem sophisticated in his presence had been acute. Female vanity, she supposed. But it had been a mistake.

Leonardo finally extracted them from his parents' overwhelming welcome with the excuse he should take Veronica up to see her villa.

'I will see you soon, *Mamma*,' he said, shepherding them both back inside whilst he retrieved Veronica's luggage, and her sunglasses, at the same time. 'After I've got Veronica settled in I'll come back down and you can tell me all the gossip.'

His mother called out something from the hotel foyer in Italian. His reply was in Italian also. Despite only knowing limited Italian, Veronica gleaned it was about dinner tonight.

'Haven't you been home for a while?' she asked as

he handed over her sunglasses, which she popped into her shoulder bag. Their eyes met again and something lurched inside her. He just stared at her for a long moment, and she stared right back, thinking how beautiful he was. Not just handsome. Beautiful.

Oh, dear…

'It's been a month since my last visit,' he said at last.

Not so very long ago, Veronica thought. She'd been imagining it must have been much longer, judging by the prodigious joy of his parents' welcome. Clearly, Leonardo was the apple of his *mamma's* and *papa's* eyes.

'This way,' he said, then took off through the paved pergola, pulling her case behind him. Veronica had to hurry to keep up with him, his stride fast and long.

'It was my father's seventy-fifth birthday,' he tossed over his shoulder. 'It was also the weekend before Laurence died. Now, watch your step on this path. It's very steep but it's the quickest way up to your villa from here. There's another road for deliveries and such, but you have to drive a fair way round to get to it, and I don't keep a car on the island.'

It *was* steep, but she was fit and didn't have much trouble with the incline, or the rather uneven stone steps. Clearly, they'd been there a long time, as had the inhabitants of this island. Franco had given her a history lesson this morning during her sightseeing tour, telling her how the Roman emperor Tiberius had moved to Capri ages ago and had used the Blue Grotto as his private swimming pool. She'd possibly heard the same story when she'd been here before as a tourist but she'd long forgotten it. But she hadn't forgotten how impressed she was by all the beautiful white villas which dotted the island. Now one of them belonged to *her*. For a while, at least.

Her eyes lifted but the villa was hidden from view by a grove of olive trees. She could just glimpse the roof, which had terracotta tiles just like the Hotel Fabrizzi.

'Did you see Laurence that weekend?' she asked, glad to return her attention to the reason why she was here. Which wasn't to go gaga over Leonardo but to find out all she could about her father.

'I did,' was all he said.

'And?' she prompted.

'I've been trying to recall what we talked about. I knew you'd ask me,' he added with a wry glance over his shoulder.

'And?'

He stopped walking and turned to face her. 'It's difficult to remember. We spent many hours together over the last few years, Laurence and I. He taught me to play chess. But I never could beat him. He was way too good.'

'I've never played chess.'

'It's not an easy game to master,' he said, and started walking up the steps again, this time by her side rather than in front.

'Do you like red wine?'

'Not really.'

'Laurence was a red wine buff. He has the most incredible cellar.'

'I noticed he left you his wine collection in his will. Have you collected it yet?'

'No need. You're selling me the villa, remember?'

'Oh, yes. Yes, of course. I forgot. Oh!' Veronica exclaimed in surprise as the villa came into view.

It wasn't what she'd been imagining. Somehow she'd been picturing a smaller version of the Hotel Fabrizzi. But it wasn't like that at all. Yes, it was mainly white. And, yes, the roof tiles were terracotta. But that was where any resemblance ended. The building was rectangular, and all on the one level, with a cloistered veranda which ran the entire length at the front. Beyond this shaded area, the main wall of the house had a lot of sliding glass doors with no obvious front door.

'Come,' Leonardo said, and led her up a small cement ramp onto the wonderfully cool veranda. Once there, Veronica stopped and turned to gaze out at the Mediterranean.

'Oh, Leonardo,' she said with a sigh of both amazement and contentment. The olive grove stopped one looking down and perhaps having the magnificent vista spoiled by the sight of buses, towns and tourists. All you could see from where she was standing was crystal blue water all the way to the horizon, with just the occasional sailboat or yacht, which hardly seemed to be moving. Everything was peaceful, soothing and, oh, so beautiful.

'Perhaps now you understand why I want to buy this place.'

'Yes indeed,' she said, aware that he'd moved to stand close to her, so close that she could smell his aftershave, or his cologne, or whatever that wonderful scent was which emanated from his skin. She'd smelt it before in the car but had done her best to ignore the effect it had on her.

Ignoring it again, she turned and looked up at him.

'And if I decide not to sell it to you?'

For a split second, anger zoomed into his eyes. But

then he laughed. 'You can't afford not to. The taxes on this place will be considerable.'

'Not so considerable if I can prove I'm Laurence's biological daughter.'

'And how do you plan to do that? He's been cremated, according to his wishes. You would need his DNA.'

'There must be something of his DNA in this place. A hairbrush, perhaps? Or a toothbrush?'

'Perhaps…'

'Don't look so worried, Leonardo. I *will* sell you the villa, but only after I've got what I came here to find out.'

'Which is what, exactly?'

'What my father looked like, for starters. There was a small article about him on the Internet, but no photos. Mum didn't have any photos, either. But, more importantly, I want to find out what kind of man he was.'

CHAPTER EIGHT

LEONARDO LOOKED DEEP into Veronica's lovely violet eyes and wondered if she'd be happy with what she found out. Laurence's looks wouldn't present a problem, since he had been a male version of her. But Laurence hadn't always been an easy man to warm to.

He'd been somewhat introverted, for starters, a typical scientist. Brilliant, but not the most sensitive of men. Leonardo imagined that as a young man emotions were not something Laurence had been familiar with.

His obsessive love for his wife must have thrown him for a loop. Because it clearly hadn't been in Laurence's nature to love like that. Her death had derailed him for a long time. Ruth had been the more social of the pair. She'd loved going to parties and entertaining at home.

It was obvious Laurence had just gone along with her wishes to keep her happy. After she'd gone, he'd sunk into a deep depression and had refused to accept any invitations, other than at Christmas, when Leonardo's *mamma* would force him to come down to the Hotel Fabrizzi for Christmas dinner. Even then, he'd been a right misery, leaving the table as soon as it was polite and sitting by himself, not talking to anyone.

Leonardo couldn't help having felt sorry for him,

priding himself on having been the person to drag Laurence out of his mourning. Every time he'd come home to visit his parents, he'd made the effort to visit him up at his villa, their friendship deepening when Leonardo had broken his ankle rock climbing a couple of years back and had come home to recuperate. Laurence had become frustrated with watching Leonardo struggle up the path on crutches to visit him and had insisted he move in with him until his ankle healed.

It was during that time together that their real friendship had begun, Leonardo having confided to Laurence over a bottle of wine one night how devastated he had been when he'd been forced to retire early from competitive skiing. No one in his family had ever understood how upset he'd been at the time. His parents had simply been pleased that he was no longer risking his neck on the slopes. Uncle Stephano had been of a similar mind-set, saying there was just as much satisfaction in succeeding in business as in sport.

None of them had had a clue.

But Laurence had. He'd understood totally, his empathy coming as a surprise.

'There is nothing worse for a man, Leonardo,' he'd said gently, 'than to have a goal snatched away from him, right when it is within reach. I know how that feels. I was on the verge of making a huge scientific discovery when all my funding for that particular research was suddenly cancelled. There was nothing I could do at the time. It was at the start of my career and I had no reputation to fall back on. I felt quite suicidal. Fortunately, I met Ruth around that time, and she made me see that there was more to life than science. One day, my boy, you will find a new dream, one which you can fulfil. Meanwhile, try to enjoy what you have, which is a lot.'

It had been sound advice. Looking back, Leonardo could see that their mutual confidences had resulted in an affection for each other that was unconditional. Leonardo had accepted Laurence's flaws, and vice versa. It had made for an ease of companionship which hadn't required the usual male tendency to try to impress. With Laurence, Leonardo had been able to be himself. He missed that.

'Laurence was a good man, but he was basically a loner,' he told Veronica, couching his words carefully. 'Most scientists are, I would imagine. Their work is a huge part of their life. Ruth used to get him to socialise. She liked entertaining and having guests to stay. But after she died he reverted to type. *Mamma* often invited him to dinner and to parties but he usually declined, except at Christmas. I guess I knew him better than anyone on Capri. He was very open with me. But, even then, it's obvious he had his secrets.'

'You're talking about me,' she said.

'Yes. You came as a shock, I can tell you.' In more ways than one. Over the phone she'd come across as brusque and spinsterish, so he'd been expecting a plain woman. But Veronica was anything but plain. She was utterly gorgeous. Leonardo suspected that he would have difficulty keeping his hands off. Already he wanted to run his fingers through her hair, to pull her to him and kiss her until she forgot all about what her father had been like. Leonardo knew he could make women forget all sorts of things, especially once he got them into bed. Make himself forget too. Sex soothed the dissatisfied beast in him. That, and gazing out at this hypnotic and wonderfully relaxing view.

Leonardo turned to gaze out across the sea for a long moment. Soon Laurence's villa—and this view—would be his. But until then he'd have to make do with other methods of relaxation.

He turned back to face Veronica with his most charming smile in place, the one which always melted the ladies and made it oh, so easy when he came across a female he fancied. And he fancied this one. More than he had in a long time, Leonardo conceded. She actually reminded him of a girl he'd come across one night many years ago. A girl very similar to Veronica in looks. A girl who'd caught his eye but who'd rejected his drunken invitation with the disdain it had probably deserved.

She'd been Australian too, he suddenly recalled.

His brows drew together as he stared at her again. Surely not?

His eyes searched hers, then travelled down her delectable body and up again. It was a long time ago, and he'd never known her name. All he'd known was that she was Australian and that she'd worked as a masseuse at a neighbouring ski resort. Sven had raved about her and asked her to one of their after-competition parties. Leonardo's retirement party, as it had turned out.

'This might seem an odd question,' he said, 'but did you ever work as a masseur in a ski resort in Switzerland? About seven or eight years ago, it would have been...'

Veronica's stomach flipped right over. She hadn't expected him to recognise her. Not on such a brief acquaintance so many years ago. They hadn't even been properly introduced.

But it seemed he had recognised her. Or almost had. What to do? Lie, or tell the truth?

She did so hate lies. Jerome had lied to her. A lot.

'I didn't think you'd recognise me,' she said simply. 'It was so long ago.'

He blinked his surprise, then smiled a rather rueful smile. 'That's how you knew I was a skier,' he said.

'Yes,' she agreed. Not to mention a playboy.

'Why didn't you tell me we'd met before?' he demanded to know, not angrily, but in a rather puzzled tone.

'I thought you might find the circumstances... embarrassing.'

He laughed. Not a loud, in-your-face belly laugh. Or an amused chuckle. More of a harsh bark.

'I admit, it wasn't one of my finer moments.'

'Really? I got the impression it was your usual *après ski* behaviour. None of the other people there seemed surprised.'

'I can't say I noticed. I was very drunk, Veronica. My career as a downhill racer had ended that day and I didn't take it well. One injury too many, I was told,' he added with a flash of remembered pain in his eyes.

She just stood there in a stiff silence, not prepared to excuse his behaviour that night so easily.

He laughed again, this time with a flash of dry humour. 'I can still remember what you said to me. *In your dreams, mate.*'

'Yes, well, when I go to bed with a guy,' she said rather tartly, 'I like to have his total attention. I'm not big on sharing.' And wasn't that the truth!

'Believe it or not, I am usually a one-woman-at-a-time man.'

'If you say so.'

He smiled a crooked smile. 'You must have a very bad opinion of me. First, from that night. And then from what I told you about the business today in Rome.'

Veronica didn't want to offend the man, but she was way past letting him whitewash his behaviour. It galled her to think he imagined she would fall for his 'poor little me' act.

'Leonardo,' she said firmly. 'Let's not pretend. Your reputation precedes you. It always has, even back in your downhill racing days. You're a player. You change your girlfriends as often as you do your clothes. I've seen dozens of photos of you on social media. But never with the same girl on your arm.'

His eyebrows lifted, his dark eyes glittering with the most irritating satisfaction.

'You checked me out on the Internet?'

Veronica heaved an exasperated sigh. Trust him to take her admission as a measure of sexual interest.

'Of course I did,' she told him in a matter-of-fact manner. 'I'm not a fool, Leonardo. I wanted to know what kind of man you were these days. I wanted to see if you could be trusted.'

'And?' He still didn't seem offended or worried, that twinkle staying in his eyes.

'As a businessman, your reputation is spotless.'

'But not as a boyfriend,' he said with laughter in his eyes.

'Well…'

'Come, come—don't quibble. Australians are well known for being straight shooters. Tell me what you think of me as a boyfriend.'

Veronica straightened her spine. 'I would say you

weren't a very good bet in that regard. Not if a woman wanted commitment.'

'That would depend on the woman,' he countered. 'I have no objection to commitment when the time— and the woman—is right. But then, not every woman is looking for commitment. Take you, for instance…'

'What? *Me?*'

'Yes, you.'

'What about me?' she demanded to know, angling her head to one side as she glared up at him.

He smiled. 'You are in your late twenties and have no one serious in your life. Yet you are a very beautiful woman. I can only conclude that you have chosen to stay—what is the term?—footloose and fancy free.'

Veronica hadn't blushed in years and she didn't blush now. But she felt quite hot inside her body, the kind of heat which came from being turned on. He was turning her on, this devilishly handsome Italian, with his verbal foreplay and his suggestive smiles.

All of a sudden she thought about what it would be like to have sex with him. Would he be as good a lover as he obviously thought he was?

Yes, she decided, a decidedly erotic shiver rippling down her spine.

Sex wasn't something that had ever been that important to Veronica. It was the romance she enjoyed. The love. Orgasms for her had always been in short supply, even with Jerome, who'd been more than competent in bed. But he hadn't been all that passionate.

Naturally not, she thought bitterly. His passion—and his love—had lain elsewhere.

Veronica stared up into Leonardo's dark, sexy eyes and just knew *he'd* be passionate in bed. Passionate, uninhibited and extremely imaginative. There wouldn't be a form of foreplay or a sexual position he hadn't tried *and* revelled in. Any man who could have offered a threesome so casually was into anything. Orgies as well, no doubt.

Such thoughts made it difficult to speak at all, let alone find the right reply. Veronica licked her dry lips, then swallowed.

'I haven't been lucky when it comes to men,' she said quite truthfully.

'That is sad. But you are still young. There is no need to panic yet.'

Now it was her turn to laugh. 'That's a matter of opinion. It seems only yesterday that I was twenty. Now, in two years, I'll be thirty.'

'You wish to get married and have children?'

Veronica shrugged. Once upon a time, she would have said yes in a heartbeat. Now, she wasn't so sure. Marriage didn't seem as straightforward as it once had. She suspected that falling in love again would be difficult for her, for starters. And, without love, marriage was out of the question.

'Only if I meet the right man,' she said. *Which certainly won't be someone like you*, she thought, despite the desire Leonardo could evoke in her with shocking ease.

'When you sell me this villa,' he replied, 'You will be rich. And men will be chasing you like mad. Possibly not the right kind of man, though, so you will have to be careful. Come,' he said, and retrieved a key from one of the large pots full of geraniums that sat along the sunny edge of the veranda. 'Time for you to see your inheritance from the inside.'

CHAPTER NINE

'DON'T LOOK SO WORRIED,' Leonardo said as he inserted the key into the lock of one of the sliding glass doors. 'We don't have a crime problem on Capri. Perhaps a little pickpocketing, occasionally, but not serious crime. Laurence always kept a key in that pot so that Carmelina could get in when he wasn't around.'

'Carmelina?'

'One of my sisters. She used to clean for Laurence. And shop. I asked her to go through the place this week and stock up with food. And, no, you do not have to pay her. She was happy to do it.'

'That was very kind of her. Do you have her number? If she speaks English I would like to thank her.'

'Everyone in my family speaks English. And you don't have to ring her. You can thank her when you see her tonight. At dinner.'

'Oh, yes. Dinner...'

Dinner tonight with his family was going to be a trial, she thought. But not as much of a trial as handling Leonardo's disturbing presence right here and now. She needed a break from his overwhelmingly attractive persona so that she could get a grip on her treacherously excited body. Veronica had the awful suspicion that if she let him stay with her any longer she might do something foolish. Once they went inside together, they would be alone. In this gorgeous house. With bedrooms and beds. She didn't trust herself. *Or* him. Not that he would force himself upon her. She didn't think that. But it was obvious Leonardo would not waste time when he fancied a girl.

And he fancied her, if the looks he kept giving her were anything to go by.

'Leonardo,' she began as he slid open the first of the huge glass doors.

He swung round to set those incredibly sexy eyes upon her. 'Yes?'

'Would you mind terribly if I walked through the house without you? I just want to soak it all in by myself. And I really do need to ring my mother. Let her know I've arrived and everything's okay. She worries, you see.'

Veronica knew she was babbling, but Leonardo was the sort of man who could make a woman babble. She would have to get control of that before tonight. He was sure to seat her right next to him at dinner. Already she was wondering what to wear.

His smile hinted that he understood she was slightly afraid to be alone with him. Or maybe she was just imagining it. Guilty conscience and all that.

'Let me just put your luggage inside,' he replied, and turned to where he'd left it.

Panic almost had her screaming at him to leave it, but she held her tongue just in time, instead dredging up the cool smile she'd used on men for the past three years but which was in danger of deserting her. With Leonardo she wanted just to smile fatuously at him and agree with everything he suggested. She'd already agreed to let him take her sightseeing tomorrow. In a helicopter, no less.

Helicopters frightened the life out of her. She didn't like the idea that if the engine conked out and the rotor blades stopped you'd drop like a stone. No hope of gliding down to a soft landing. Not that you could do that in a big plane. Maybe she could suggest tonight over dinner that they cruise around in a boat instead. Not a small sailing boat. One with a big crew, to stop him from pouncing once they were at sea.

As soon as her black wheelie case was safely inside the enormous living area, he took her gently by the shoulders and gazed down into her ever-widening eyes. Lord, was he going to kiss her?

He didn't. She just wished he had. Instead, he shook his head at her, as if he knew what was going on in *her* head.

'You should have a rest this afternoon,' he advised. 'Dinner with my family is not a quick event. *Mamma* will want to impress you with all her best dishes, so don't eat too much before you come. I shall be here to pick you up at seven.'

'What…what should I wear?'

He shrugged. 'Nothing formal. If you wear a dress, then bring a wrap. Or a jacket. The evenings start warm but cool down quickly. *Arrivederci*, Veronica.'

And then he did kiss her. Not a big, swooping, passionate kiss. Just a peck, really. But on her lips. A light, lovely kiss which made her long for more. And then he was gone, not looking back once as he'd stridden away from her, his long legs carrying him down off the veranda and swiftly out of sight.

Veronica just stood there for long moment, staring blindly after him, not breathing, not thinking. Only yearning. No…craving. She *craved* Leonardo Fabrizzi. It was a stunning realisation. Because she'd never craved a man like that before. She knew it wasn't love she was feeling. It was lust making her heart thud and her lungs ache from not breathing. She gasped in then, sucking in the gloriously fresh air, clearing her light-headedness to a degree.

Crossing her arms, she hugged herself, then turned and stared through the glass doors at the view of the sea once more, using its soothing quality to find some common sense, asking herself what did it matter if she lusted after this man? What would it matter if she even had sex with him? It didn't have to lead anywhere. It *wouldn't* lead anywhere. Anyone who knew anything about Leonardo Fabrizzi would know that.

A slow smile spread across Veronica's face as she thought about Leonardo. What a devil he was. But a very charming devil. And sexy as hell. A girl would have to be dead to resist him.

'And I'm far from dead,' she said aloud as she un-wrapped her arms and spread them wide. 'I'm over Jerome. I'm here on the gorgeous Isle of Capri. And I'm about to inspect my father's equally gorgeous house!'

CHAPTER TEN

IT *WAS* GORGEOUS. The living area, especially. It was open plan, but not overly modern, though it did have all the mod cons. The floors were Italian marble in swirls of white and grey, the rugs very colourful. The furniture was an eclectic mixture of stuff one might see in an English home, the two sofas rather formal and chintzy, the armchairs large, squashy and very country. The dining table was oval-shaped, and made of an almost black wood, with six matching high-back chairs around it, the seats covered in green velvet. In the middle of the table sat the most glorious green glass…thing. Not a bowl. Or a vase. More of a sculptured shape with no visible purpose other than to be beautiful.

Possibly Murano glass, Veronica decided, having briefly visited Venice and the island of Murano during the Italy-in-a-week tour she'd undertaken when she'd been twenty-one. Whatever it was, she loved it. Had her father chosen it?

Thinking of her father sent Veronica hurrying over to the far wall where there was a selection of photos arranged on the mantelpiece above the fireplace. At last, she would see what her father looked like.

Her eyes immediately went to the wedding photo,

which was black-and-white and showed the bride dressed in a long, straight gown and a heavy lace veil which had gone out of fashion aeons ago. She was short, slim and pretty in a soft blonde way. The groom was very tall, dark and handsome. Strong looking, with an air about him that was impressive at first glance until you looked a second time. His face was turned towards his bride, his expression both loving and vulnerable. Here was a man very deeply in love, with a love that surprised him.

Turning the frame over, she saw there was writing on the back:

Laurence and Ruth
On our wedding day, March 1968

Twenty-two years before I was conceived, Veronica thought.

The other photos showed them growing older, some of them alone and others in groups. Laurence had aged very well, keeping his thick, lustrous hair even when it had turned grey. His wife had faded with time, growing frailer with the years. But her smile remained bright and warm, her eyes loving whenever they were lifted to her husband. Which was often. He in turn always had his hands on her somewhere, either on her shoulders or around her waist. His body language was both protective and possessive. Yet not in any way threatening. Despite Ruth being the more fragile looking, Veronica suspected it was she who had worn the trousers in their relationship. Only one photo showed the colour of her father's eyes. They were, as everyone had pointed out, violet, just like hers. They were shaped like hers too.

It pleased her, then made her sad.

She would have loved to know her father when he had still been alive. Instead, all she could do was pick over other people's memories of him. And stare at old photos. Suddenly, the tears came, rolling down her cheeks and dripping off her nose. Thankfully, they didn't last long, Veronica pulling herself together by turning and looking through the mainly glass wall at the view beyond.

What *was* it about that view? It was only water, after all. Did the Mediterranean possess some kind of magic? Or was it Capri that was magical?

Whatever, it did the trick, bringing a sense of peace to her soul and an acceptance of the situation. At least she *had* some sense of her father's memories now. And photos. And this lovely villa. For a while, anyway. What a shame she could not live here permanently.

'Don't start wishing for the moon, Veronica,' she told herself sternly, then turned and went to discover the rest of her father's home.

Two hours later, after taking more photos than she could count, Veronica sent them to her mother's phone then rang her.

'Hel…lo?' came a very fuzzy voice after several rings.

'Oh, dear,' Veronica said, wincing. 'I've woken you up. Sorry, Mum. I forgot about the time difference.'

'No trouble,' she said, sounding a little more awake. 'What time is it?'

'Er…just after four. In the morning. What's up?'

'I'm here on Capri, in the villa.'

'What's it like? Not a crumbling ruin, I hope.'

Veronica laughed. 'Hardly. I've taken heaps of photos and sent them to you. Have a look and see for yourself.'

'Just a sec. Oh, yes. I've got them. Oh…wow! That is some view. Is that the view from the villa or somewhere else?'

'No, that's the view from the villa.'

'No wonder the place is worth heaps. That view alone is worth millions.'

'I agree. And the villa is fantastic.'

'Yes, it's lovely. Not very Italian-looking inside.'

'No. The decor is more English but the bones are Italian. Lots of marble on the floors and in the bathrooms. And the fireplace is very Italian. The kitchen is modern, despite the wooden benches. *And* the huge cooker.'

'Four bedrooms, I notice. Yet they didn't have children.'

'Leonardo said they used to entertain when his wife was still alive.'

'What's he like, this Leonardo chap?'

Veronica swallowed. To lie or not to lie? She didn't want her mother worrying about her. And she might, if she said he was utterly gorgeous and she fancied him like mad.

'Oh, he's a typical Italian. You know the type. Very charming.'

'And very good-looking,' her mother said, startling her.

'How would you know that?'

'After you left I looked him up on the Internet. He's quite the playboy, isn't he?'

'Yes,' Veronica admitted. 'But harmless, once you know the species.'

Her mother laughed. 'Remember that Brazilian exchange student who chased after you during your first year at university.'

Veronica groaned. 'How could I forget?'

'He got you in the end, though, didn't he?'

'Mum! How on earth did you know that? I never said.'

'You always did like guys who refused to take no for an answer.'

She did, she supposed. Jerome had been like that. He'd pursued her like mad. She hadn't really wanted to go out with a doctor. Certainly not a surgeon. She knew the hours they worked. But she'd given in after the tenth lot of roses had arrived, and then she'd fallen in love with him, agreeing to marry him in a few short weeks. She'd never suspected Jerome had had a secret agenda. Never suspected anything.

'Has he made a pass at you yet?' her mother asked slyly.

Now she really did have to lie. 'No. He said something about a girlfriend in Rome. Though I *am* going to his family's place for dinner tonight. They own a hotel just below the villa. It's only a short walk down some stone steps. But first I must have a sleep. I'm exhausted.' And hungry, she suddenly realised.

'You might be exhausted but you sound happy. Happier than you've been in years. I was angry with Laurence for putting you in his will at first but now I'm grateful. This inheritance has been good for you, love. You're sounding like the girl you were before you met Jerome.'

Veronica blinked. 'Don't you mean before Jerome was killed?'

'No. I mean before you *met* that bastard.'

Veronica was truly taken aback. 'But I thought you liked Jerome. I mean…before we found out about him.'

'I just pretended to like him. For your sake. I always thought he was up himself. And so was his family. Talk about snobs!'

'They were on the snobbish side,' Veronica admitted.

'They thought you weren't good enough for their precious son. Little did they know he wasn't good enough for you.'

Veronica sighed.

'Now, none of that,' her mother said. 'Go back to the girl who rang me a few minutes ago. She's the girl you used to be before Jerome. She was a terrific girl who knew how to have fun. That man turned you into a try-hard. And then he turned you into a bitter cow like me.'

'Oh, Mum, you're nothing of the kind.'

'Yes, I am, and I hate myself for it. I don't know how you've put up with me all these years. The one thing I truly regret is that I didn't try to help you out of your unhappiness. To my shame, I just let you wallow in it.'

Veronica was so astonished by her mother's words she couldn't think of a thing to say.

'Of course, I liked it that you didn't have anyone else but me,' her mother confessed. 'And that you were living and working from home. I used to smugly think, *now she knows what it's like to have your trust in men destroyed*. Laurence's will was a wake-up call to me, I can tell you. When I saw how upset you were, it nearly killed me. I vowed then and there to stop being so selfish and to encourage you to get out there and make a life for yourself. I'm sure not all men are as rotten as Jerome, or that excuse for a husband I once had. There are good men out there. Men like your father. *He* was a good man. Very loving and loyal to his wife. I'm sure there is someone out there just right for you. Meanwhile, if this Leonardo makes a pass at you, then go for it, darling. He's one hot hunk.'

'Wow, Mum, I don't know what to say!'

'You don't have to say anything at all. Just accept my apology and go have some fun. Oh, and one last thing.'

'What?'

'Please don't feel you have to ring me all the time. Nothing worse than going on holiday and feeling you have to check in with your mother. But feel free to send any photos and the odd text. Okay?'

'Okay,' she agreed with a smile on her face.

CHAPTER ELEVEN

LEONARDO LEAPT UP the stone steps two a time, excited by the prospect of seeing Veronica again. And having her meet his whole family. They were excited to meet her as well, his two sisters very curious over this girl who was Laurence's biological daughter.

Carmelina had liked Laurence a lot, but then she was the one who had seen him the most, being his cleaner as well as Ruth's sometime carer. She'd been astonished by the news that he had a secret daughter, and relieved when she heard that Veronica had been conceived through IVF and not some sordid affair.

The sun had set but it was still light, a golden hue hovering on the horizon. A silvery half-moon was up as well, bathing Laurence's villa in soft moonlight.

Leonardo bounced up onto the terrace and was about to press the front doorbell when the sliding glass door opened and there stood Veronica, looking even more beautiful than she had earlier that day. Gone were the jeans and simple striped top and in their place a sexy lilac sundress which left her shoulders bare, the halter neckline hinting at just enough cleavage.

Across her right forearm lay a black lacy cardigan.

'I won't need to bring a bag, will I?' she asked, looking up at him with sparkling eyes, their violet colour darker than they had been in the sunshine. Dark and sexier.

'Not on my account,' he replied with a smile. *Dio*, but she was delicious. Her hair was still up. Not severely but softly, with dark curls kissing her pale cheeks and throat. Her mouth was glossed in a plum colour, her eyes shadowed in a silvery grey which matched the moonlight. He couldn't wait to bring her home after dinner and take her to bed. She wouldn't say no. He could already feel the heat sizzling from her skin. Could feel his own as well, his hot Italian blood charging through his veins.

Thank God he was wearing loosely tailored slacks. They stopped his erection from being obvious. Leonardo didn't like being obvious.

She smiled back at him. 'I'll just lock up and put the key in that ridiculously obvious pot. I hope this building and its contents are insured,' she added as she did just that.

'They are,' he assured her, amused by her concern over security.

'Did you have a good look at everything?' he asked her as he took her elbow and guided her from the terrace.

'Yes. It's a lovely house. I had a look at some photos of Laurence as well. I do take after him, don't I?'

'You do. In looks. But you're much nicer.'

She halted at the top of the stone steps. 'What do you mean? Wasn't my father a nice person?'

Leonardo instantly regretted his tactless words. 'He was a very nice person,' he said, regrouping quickly. 'But you're even nicer.'

'Oh…' Her cheeks coloured a little, her eyes blinking with the most charming embarrassment. 'How can you say that? You don't really know me.'

'I am a quick judge of people. And a good judge, I believe.'

'You weren't with that girl in Rome,' she shot back, startling him into laughter.

'True. There are times when my hormones lead me astray.'

'I think your hormones lead you astray a lot,' she said drily, making him wonder if perhaps she would say no to him tonight. He hoped not, because he wanted this girl more and more with each passing moment.

'Come,' he said, and closed his fingers more tightly around her elbow. '*Mamma* is champing at the bit to feed you.'

'I don't think I could eat another bite,' Veronica whispered to Leonardo a couple of hours later.

'Try,' he whispered back.

'I hope you don't think it rude of me, Veronica,' Sophia said rather loudly from where she was sitting at the end of the table furthest from them. 'But I must ask you—your mother…why she not just get married if she wanted a *bambino*?'

'*Mamma,*' Leonardo chided with a wry shake of his handsome head. 'That *is* a rather rude question.'

'No, no,' Veronica said straight away, not wanting to offend Sophia, who was really a lovely person. Veronica already liked her enormously. She liked *all* of Leonardo's family. And there were twelve of them sitting at the table under the pergola that evening. Alberto and Sophia had three children, Veronica had learned when introduced properly. Elena was the oldest, followed by Carmelina and then Leonardo. Elena was married to Franco, the taxi driver, and they had three children. Marco was eleven, Bianca was nine with the youngest, Bruno, a precocious seven. Carmelina was the only shy one of the family. She was married to Alfonso, who worked at the Hotel Fabrizzi as a handyman-cum-gardener. They had a son, Luca, who was ten and a daughter, Daniele, who was eight.

'It is a fair question,' Veronica went on. She presumed Leonardo had explained how Laurence had come to be a sperm donor, but even he didn't know the reasons behind her mother's decision to have a baby that way. 'My mother actually was married when she was younger. But her husband was not a good man. He gambled away all their money, treated her badly then left her to run away with another woman. A rich widow. She had a nervous breakdown and lost her job. In the end she had nothing and could only get work as a housekeeper. She was very bitter about men and vowed never to trust one ever again. But as she got older she desperately wanted a baby.

'Around this time she was employed by Laurence. He was in Australia doing research at the Sydney University. His job came with a large house in nearby Glebe, along with a live-in housekeeper. That was Mum. She liked Laurence, said he was a decent man. They became friendly and one day she confided in him her plan to have a baby by artificial insemination.'

'And that was when Laurence offered his sperm instead of some stranger's,' Leonardo intervened. 'He didn't want to risk the baby having a bad gene, like Ruth apparently had. That was the reason Ruth didn't have children, by the way. She was worried they would inherit her bad gene. But Laurence knew his genes were fine.'

'Better than fine,' Leonardo's father said with a big smile on his face, his accent much stronger than Leonardo's. He waved his arms around a lot. 'Just look at the beautiful girl he produced. He would have been so proud of you, Veronica. You are *molto bella*. Your *mamma* must be very happy that she listened to Laurence.'

Other members of the family chimed in with their compliments as well.

Veronica tried not to blush. But, really, the whole family had been gushing and fussing over her all evening. She loved the attention but it was a bit overwhelming. She hoped and prayed that both Elena and Carmelina would get up and go soon. Unfortunately, the children didn't seem at all tired, and tomorrow was Saturday, after all. Not a school day. She couldn't claim she was wilting, either, having had a long nap this afternoon.

The beginning of a yawn took her by surprise.

'Tired?' Leonardo murmured in her ear.

'No,' she confessed with a soft sigh. 'Not really.'

'Good,' he said quietly so that only she could hear. 'I will tell everyone you have jet lag and need to go home to bed.'

Veronica was tempted, but when she turned her head and saw the devilish glint in his eye she found herself not wanting to do as he obviously wanted her to do. Not yet. As madly attractive as she found him, as fast as her heart was beating, her days of being a pushover with the opposite sex were well and truly over.

'No,' she said with a coolness which surprised even her. 'No, I don't want to do that. I'm not fond of lying.'

'A little white lie won't hurt anyone,' he grumbled. Clearly, he wasn't used to being thwarted.

'That's a matter of opinion,' Veronica retorted. 'Your mother would be offended. She's gone to a lot of trouble with this meal.'

'Very well, but be warned—I can't protect you from *Mamma's* never-ending questions if you stay.'

'What was that?' Sophia immediately jumped in. 'Are you talking about me, Leonardo?'

'Veronica was just complimenting you on the food, *Mamma*,' he said, showing Veronica how smoothly *he* could lie. 'She said you have gone to a lot of trouble.'

Sophia looked very pleased. 'She is welcome.'

Veronica smiled at her, glad now that she had stayed. But she almost wished she'd said yes to Leonardo's suggestion when Sophia went on to ask her a multitude of questions about her life back in Sydney, finally asking if there was a boyfriend waiting for her at home. It was a reasonable question, she supposed, but she was always reluctant to discuss her personal life. Or lack of one. It was a relief when Leonardo answered for her.

'Not at the moment, *Mamma*,' he said. 'I asked Veronica just that earlier today and she claimed not to be lucky when it came to men. Perhaps she will be luckier now that she is an heiress,' he added with a slight edge in his voice.

Sophia rattled off something exasperated in Italian before apologising, then returning to English. 'I said you would not need the money to be attractive to men,' she told Veronica.

Veronica had a feeling she'd just been lied to, as

everyone else at the table exchanged knowing looks. She'd heard Leonardo's name in there somewhere, not her own name.

'She might be divorced,' the precocious Bruno suddenly piped up.

An embarrassed silence settled on the table for a long moment.

'There's a thought,' Leonardo muttered. '*Are* you divorced, Veronica?'

CHAPTER TWELVE

SHE BLINKED UP at him, startled, he thought, by his question.

'Absolutely not,' came her firm reply. 'I've never been married.'

Leonardo wasn't sure why he was relieved at this news.

Why was he so pleased to hear Veronica wasn't in that category?

He had no idea. Neither did he wish to worry about it.

'But you do wish to get married?' Elena asked her.

Leonardo noticed Veronica's hesitation to answer. But then she smiled and said, 'Yes, of course. If I ever meet a man I can both love and trust.'

Ah, Leonardo thought. She *had* been burnt in the past. And burnt quite badly, by the sound of things.

'You should marry an Italian,' Elena continued. 'They make very good husbands.' And she gave Franco a loving glance.

My sister is as bad as my mother, Leonardo decided. *Always matchmaking.*

'I think it is time I took Veronica home,' he said, and stood up abruptly. 'She has had a long day, and I'm taking her sightseeing by helicopter tomorrow morning.'

He knew that mentioning this would stop any objections to his escorting Veronica home. His mother and sisters would be satisfied with this news and could plan further matchmaking in their absence.

Not that any of it would work. Firstly, he didn't really want to get married just yet. And, even if he did, he wasn't about to marry an Australian girl who would be going home soon, never to return. Yes, he found Veronica extremely attractive. And, yes, he aimed to get her into bed before the weekend was out. Before this night was out, actually. But once she sold him the villa that would be the end of things. She would return to her life in Sydney and he would go on as before.

Leonardo looked down at Veronica who hadn't made a move to stand up. Surely *she* wasn't going to object?

She glanced up at him with those big violet eyes of hers, and once again it zapped between them—the sexual chemistry that had been there from their first meeting, and which he'd been trying to ignore all evening. It was impossible to ignore it any longer. It was like an electric shock, making every muscle in Leonardo's body contract as he battled to harness his desire into some semblance of control. But he knew, as surely as he knew he was on Capri, that the moment he took this glorious creature into his arms nothing would stop this night from reaching its inevitable conclusion.

And his satisfaction would be sublime!

CHAPTER THIRTEEN

VERONICA SUCKED IN her breath sharply. My God, the way he was looking at her. It was downright scary. But, oh, so exciting. And like nothing she'd ever experienced before. Jerome had never looked at her like that, as though he wanted to possess every part of her, body and soul. The thought thrilled her, then turned her on to the max.

Her lips dried as her heartbeat took off. So this was what real lust felt like—and she accepted only in that moment that this was something new to her. Yes, she'd been attracted to men before. Yes, she'd been to bed with a few. And, yes, it had been pleasant enough. But nothing to write home about. Jerome had been an improvement in the bedroom department. But then, she'd imagined herself in love with Jerome. And he'd obviously known what he was doing. He'd been in his late thirties, after all. But she'd never wanted him with this kind of passion, never felt her whole body react this way just to a look.

My God, she was on fire! She regretted putting on her wrap earlier, although she knew, deep down, that one small short-sleeved cardigan wasn't responsible for the heat gathering in every pore of her body.

'Come,' Leonardo commanded, and held out his hand to her.

Yes please, she thought with a jolt of uncharacteristic boldness. *Very* uncharacteristic. Veronica wasn't the type of girl whose focus in sex was constantly on having an orgasm. She'd always been more into how she felt about the man making love to her than if she came or not.

Not so with this man. He brought out the female animal in her, not the soul mate. She just wanted him to…

Veronica hated the F-word. But it was appropriate on this occasion. Because that was what Leonardo did to women. He didn't care about them. Or love them. He just screwed them silly till he got bored, and then he walked away.

His fingers closed around hers and he drew her slowly to her feet, then helped her slide out from behind the seat. Her knees held her upright, thank heavens, but it was a bit of touch and go. Thank heavens he kept a firm hold of her hand or she might have stumbled, a dizzying weakness having overtaken her. Veronica could feel everyone's eyes upon her. Could they see what was going on in her head? she wondered dazedly. Which was what, exactly? Nothing that children should know. Her mind was filling with R-rated images of herself and Leonardo tumbling together naked in a bed.

There were four bedrooms in the villa. She wasn't sure which one figured in her fantasy, her mind more on what they were doing, not where they were.

Somehow Veronica managed to say goodnight to everyone, as well as thank Sophia for the wonderful meal. She endured several hugs and kisses, and then Leonardo was leading her away—not hurrying, she noticed, for which she was both grateful and irritated. He obviously wasn't feeling the same urgency she was.

'I've remembered one of the things I talked to Laurence about that last weekend,' he said as he led her along the gravel path that led to the stone steps. '*Mamma's* infernal matchmaking brought it all back to me.'

'Oh?' was all she could manage in reply, until guilt arrived. What on earth was wrong with her? She'd come to Capri to find out about her father, not crave hot sex with the executor of his will!

She stopped and turned to face Leonardo. 'What was it?' she asked, doing her best not to think how handsome he was in the moonlight. And how sexy.

'I complained to him about *Mamma* going on and on about my getting married and having a family. *Papa* was just as bad that weekend. He said he wanted me to have a son to carry on our family name. The only other Fabrizzi alive is my uncle Stephano and he doesn't have any children. *Papa* said it was my duty to get married and have a family.'

'But you don't *want* to get married,' she pointed out. Leonardo was a playboy. Always had been. Always would be. Hadn't his parents got that yet?

He pulled a face. 'I admit the idea of marriage doesn't appeal at the moment. I like my life the way it is for now.'

'Have you told them that?'

'Not exactly. I want to please them, but...' He shrugged, as though the decision was out of his hands. He turned and they headed up the ancient steps, Leonardo recapturing her hand.

As much as his touch sent an exciting charge shooting up her arm, this time Veronica refused to be totally distracted by it.

'What did Laurence say?' she asked. 'Did he give you any advice?'

'He said that I would change my mind about marriage when the right girl came along. He said falling in love did that to even the most confirmed bachelor.'

'That was naive of him, wasn't it?' came her slightly caustic comment. Because Veronica wasn't fooled by this man's charm, or his avid attentions. She doubted that Leonardo would ever meet the right girl. He was programmed to fall in lust but never in love.

He said nothing for a few seconds, not turning to face her till they reached the top of the steep incline.

'You are very cynical. Some man hurt you, didn't he? And, no, I don't want to hear the sordid details. I hate it when girls feel they have to tell you every moment of every bad relationship they've had. It is usually man-bashing. And boring. And turns me right off. Not that anything you said would turn me off tonight,' he added with a smile so criminally sexy that her toes curled up in her shoes. 'You could tell me you were the secret mistress to an Arab sheikh and I would still want to take you to bed.'

How did she keep a straight face? Somehow, she managed. Because she needed to show this arrogant Italian playboy that she had his measure. And was a match for him in every way.

'That's an interesting thought,' she said with brilliant nonchalance. 'No. I'm not the secret mistress of *a* sheikh. There are actually two of them. Mine are into horse racing. Plus riding of another kind,' she added with a saucy glance. 'And, my, they do keep me busy.'

It was only a momentary coup, but it was worth it to see his eyes widen in shock for a few seconds. But all too soon he realised that she was pulling his leg. His laugh was rueful.

'You are a devil in disguise, aren't you?'

'Not quite as much as you, Leonardo. But, yes, I do like being footloose and fancy free at the moment.' Lord, this lying business could get to be a habit! 'Though I do intend to get married. Eventually.'

'When you meet the right man,' he pointed out in an echo of what she'd said earlier.

'Exactly. Which I'm sorry to say is not you, Leonardo. I prefer my future husband to be a little less... travelled.'

He grinned. 'But not your lovers.'

'No. Not my lovers. There is something to be said for experience in the bedroom. Practice does make perfect, I've found.'

His eyebrows lifted. 'So you *have* had a sheikh or two in your bed?'

She gave him a coy glance. 'I'm not a kiss-and-tell kind of girl.'

'Thank heaven for small mercies,' he said, surprising her constantly with how well he spoke English, knowing all the right phrases and idioms. 'But let me remind you that I haven't even kissed you yet. Not a proper kiss, anyway.'

'No. You haven't.'

'Should I remedy that?'

'Not out here,' she said with a flash of panic, aware suddenly that she wasn't ready yet for their verbal foreplay to become reality. Maybe she would never be ready.

The way she was feeling was quite frightening. So were the images which kept popping into her head.

Veronica's hand trembled a little as she retrieved the key from the geranium pot and unlocked the sliding door. It was cooler inside. Pity *she* wasn't. She didn't turn to see if he'd followed her—because she knew instinctively he would have. Instead, she switched on the lights then walked quickly over to the kitchen area, finding safety behind the long breakfast bar before turning to face him.

'Would you like something to drink?' she asked him. 'Coffee? Tea? *Water?*' she finished drily.

His smile showed he recognised her action for the delaying tactic that it was.

'I would prefer a glass of cognac. Or a port. Laurence has a magnificent one which he used to buy by the case-load. Have you been down to Laurence's wine cellar yet?'

'No,' she admitted. 'I couldn't find it.' In truth, she hadn't really looked.

'I'll show you where it is,' he offered, and held out his hand to her again.

'I need to go to the bathroom first,' she prevaricated. Although, now she thought about it, it was the truth. Her bladder had suddenly started protesting.

Veronica dashed off to the master bedroom which had an *en suite* bathroom. When she returned to the living area a few minutes later, Leonardo was there, his left arm resting on the marble mantelpiece as he stared broodingly into the empty fireplace.

'I still can't believe Laurence is dead,' he said, glancing back up at her with touchingly sad eyes.

Veronica was quite moved by his grief.

'He should have contacted you earlier,' he went on with an angry flash in his dark eyes. 'He was your *papa*. He was your flesh and blood. It was wrong of him to keep you a secret.'

'I think so too,' she agreed with a catch in her throat. 'But it's too late now.'

'*Si*. Much too late. I do not understand what he was thinking.'

'Neither do I.'

Leonardo frowned. 'Possibly he wasn't thinking at all. He was very depressed after Ruth died. Very grumpy too, at times. But I still liked him. He was good to me when I needed him. I miss him. Terribly. As strange as it might seem, he was my best friend, despite our age difference. He was always totally honest with me. And I liked that.'

'Honesty is a good virtue in a friend,' Veronica choked out, struggling a little with this conversation. *She* would liked to have been her father's best friend too.

'I have made you sad,' Leonardo said with a combination of regret and frustration in his voice. 'I did not walk you home to make you sad. Now, no more delaying tactics,' he went on with suddenly hungry eyes. 'I don't want coffee, or cognac. Not even that port I told you about. I just want you, Veronica. Only you…'

CHAPTER FOURTEEN

ONLY ME, VERONICA thought breathlessly as she watched him remove his arm from the mantelpiece and slowly walk towards her.

He could not have said anything more perfect. Or more seductive. If ever she'd needed to be wanted the way Leonardo professed to want her, it was now.

This time, she went into his arms without hesitation. And without any more qualms. Or worries. It was as though with those impassioned words he'd blinded her to the slightly sordid reality of the situation and turned their assignation into something sweet. Romantic, even.

Her arms wound up around his neck and slowly pulled his mouth down onto hers. But within seconds of his lips meeting hers the timbre of the moment changed. Suddenly, there was nothing sweet or romantic about his kiss. Or her response to it. The inner fire which she'd been desperately trying to douse all day sprang back into life with a vengeance. It was like the most savage bush fire, the ones which scorched everything in their path. Up on tiptoe, she pressed her open mouth to his like a woman dying of thirst, with the moisture of *his* mouth her salvation. When his tongue dived deep, her lips closed around it and sucked hard. He gasped, then moaned, then lifted her up off her feet. She wrapped her legs around his waist and he carried her like that into the master bedroom. There, he threw her across the bed, his breathing ragged as he glared down at her.

'*Dio,*' he muttered, shaking his head as he kicked off his shoes and started stripping off his clothes.

Veronica tried to think. Tried to will herself to move. But her mind was all on him, on this magnificent male animal whom she wanted as she had never wanted anyone before. Her hungry gaze ogled him shamelessly as he undressed, her eyes stunned by his rapidly unfolding beauty. Naked, he was everything she'd imagined and more. Not too big or too small. No flaws. Just perfect in every way. She loved the olive colour of his skin, and the sculptured look of his stomach muscles. She loved his broad shoulders and his long, strong legs. Skier's legs. But most of all she loved the length and strength of his erection.

When she started thinking of how he would feel sliding into her she *did* move, her hands reaching up under her skirt and ripping off her panties, uncaring that she'd ruined them. A need was possessing her, a need so powerful and impassioned that there was no room for shame. Or decorum.

'Hurry,' she choked out.

For a long moment he just stood there beside the bed and stared down at her, his expression stunned. Veronica groaned with frustration, lifting her skirt up and spreading her knees.

'Just do it,' she begged, her desire now desperate. She was so turned on she feared she might come with him still standing there staring at her. 'Please, Leonardo…'

Finally, he fell upon her, entering her with little finesse, taking her hands and scooping them up above her head, holding her captive against the bed as he pounded into her. Surprisingly, she didn't come straight away, moaning and groaning as her head whipped from side to side. He kept saying things to her in Italian. Not romantic-sounding words. Hard, hot, perhaps angry, words. After what felt like for ever she came, and he came with her, their bodies shuddering together, their mouths gasping wide. Veronica squeezed her eyes shut, afraid to look into his, afraid of what she might see.

Please God, not disgust!

He let her arms go with a sound she could not identify. Whatever, it didn't sound happy.

'I did not use protection,' he growled.

She opened her eyes, not to an expression of disgust, but anger.

'You did not give me time!' he accused her in harsh tones.

He was possibly right. But she hadn't exactly put a gun to his head and forced him to have sex with her. If he'd wanted to use a condom, he could have. She opened her mouth to apologise then closed it again. Why should she say sorry? Practising safe sex was as much his responsibility as hers.

'You don't have to worry,' she shot back at him. 'I won't get pregnant.'

Veronica knew her body well and her period was due next Monday. She should have ovulated more than a week ago.

He clasped the sides of her face and glowered down at her. 'You are on the pill?' he demanded to know.

His attitude both frightened and annoyed her. If she told him she wasn't, he would probably have a conniption. Or a tantrum. She could imagine that Leonardo would have had tantrums as a boy. He was spoiled rotten. That much was clear. She hated lies, but there were times when a little white lie was the only option.

'Yes, of course,' she said. 'What do you think I am, a fool? And, whilst we're asking each other personal questions, I hope you don't make a habit of practising unsafe sex.'

'Never!' he said, looking quite offended.

'Before tonight, that is,' she pointed out archly.

It shocked Veronica how quickly her feelings for Leonardo could go from uncontrollable desire to outright dislike.

He reared up onto his elbows with a strange look on his face. Was that shock in his eyes? Or just confusion? Clearly, he wasn't used to losing control as he just had.

'I think I should go,' he said and suddenly withdrew, scrambling up off the bed and reaching for his clothes.

Tears of hurt and humiliation stung Veronica's eyes. Suddenly, she felt both used and very cheap. She must have a made a sound because he turned and saw her distress.

'No, no,' he said hurriedly, sitting back down and pulling her up into his arms again. 'You were lovely. I am just not used to acting so foolishly. It has thrown me. There was this girl once. But no,' he said with a bitter laugh. 'I will not bore you with the details. Needless to say, it is a case of once bitten, twice shy when it comes to risking an unwanted child.'

Understanding dawned. He'd been targeted once before by a gold digger, some girl who'd tried to trap him with a pregnancy.

'I would not try to trap you with a baby, Leonardo,'

she said gently, and stroked the back of his head, feeling suddenly tender towards him. Thank God she was certain there would be no unwanted pregnancy from tonight's mistake. 'It's a rotten thing for a girl to do.'

'It is.'

'Did she have a baby, this girl?'

He drew back and smiled a relieved smile. 'Happily, no. She wasn't pregnant at all. She just said she was.'

'What a wicked deception.' Veronica knew all about wicked deceptions. They scarred people. This girl had scarred Leonardo, trying to trap him into marriage before he was ready. And no doubt without love involved.

Leonardo sighed heavily, then stood up and started dressing. 'I would have married her,' he confessed as he zipped up his trousers.

'But why, if you didn't love her?'

'It is a question of honour,' he said, pulling on his shirt. 'The baby would have been mine.'

'That is a little old-fashioned, Leonardo. Honestly, an Australian man wouldn't have felt obliged to marry such a girl.'

'But to walk away from your own child,' Leonardo said, frowning. 'That is not right. I could not do that.'

'You didn't have to walk away. You could have paid child care and demanded visiting rights. Why marry when there's no love involved? To do that is not right, either.'

His smile was wry. 'Italians feel differently on the subject.'

Veronica shook her head. 'Then you are different, all right.'

'Apparently so. Now, I really must go, or *Mamma* will start getting ideas. She already likes you enormously,' he added, laughing. 'If I stay any longer she will be planning our wedding before the weekend is out.'

Veronica laughed too. 'Then you'd definitely better go.'

'I'll pick you up at ten tomorrow morning. Don't wear a dress or a skirt. We're going in a helicopter, remember?'

'Okay.'

'Ciao.'

She watched him leave, thinking that perhaps she should have told him she was afraid of helicopters. But she didn't want to sound like a scaredy-cat. She liked it that he saw her as a bit of an adventuress. Which she had been, once. She'd thought nothing of travelling to the snowfields in Europe on her own every year when she'd been doing her uni course. She would save up all year from her two part-time jobs and splurge the lot every January, backpacking from one ski resort to the next. It wasn't till the last year of her course that she'd been able to make it a working holiday, using her qualifications to get a job as a remedial masseuse at one of the top ski resorts.

That was where she'd run into Leonardo.

Who would have believed what fate had had in store for her when she'd rejected him that night? Veronica would never have imagined that she would actually have sex with Leonardo several years later. Or that she would jump into bed with him so quickly and so shamelessly. For years after the night of that party, she'd told herself firmly that she'd imagined how turned on she was at the time, and how difficult it had been to resist him. But she'd known, the moment he'd introduced himself over the phone two weeks ago, that he was the most dangerously attractive man she'd ever met.

Yes, she'd come to Capri to find out about her father. But she finally admitted that she'd also come because of Leonardo. To meet him again and see if all her sexual feelings about the man were just fantasies or the real McCoy. Well, now she had her answer, didn't she? The desires he could evoke in her—oh, so effortlessly—were real. Very real.

Not dangerous, though. Unless she did something stupid, such as fall in love with him.

Which Veronica resolved not to do. She wasn't a silly young girl any longer. She was an adult, with a wealth of experience behind her. She knew precisely what she was dealing with.

Leonardo was a playboy and a commitment-phobe. He pretended that one day he would settle down but she very much doubted it. Clearly, he didn't want to sleep with the same woman for the rest of his life. All he wanted to do with the opposite sex was have fun.

Well, that was what she wanted from him, Veronica decided. Just fun.

To want anything more would be crazy.

And she wasn't crazy. She was, however, crazy about Leonardo's body. Oh, Lord he was just so gorgeous. Her stomach lurched as she recalled how it had felt when he'd entered her. She could hardly wait till tomorrow.

Showing her Capri by helicopter wouldn't take long, Veronica imagined as she hurried inside. She had no doubt that when he brought her home afterwards he would stay for a while. Maybe even for the rest of the day. Things tonight had been so rushed. Thrilling, yes, and very satisfying. Had she ever had an orgasm like it?

All her internal muscles squeezed tight as she tried to relive the moment when she'd splintered apart in his arms. But the memory was already fading.

I needed to experience it again. And again. I don't want to ever forget.

Veronica reached the master bedroom where she stared at the indentations their bodies had made on the bed. Tomorrow, she vowed, they would not be having a quickie on top of the quilt. They would lie naked together *in* the bed. She would insist Leonardo make love to her more slowly, with plenty of adventurous foreplay. Veronica had never been into oral sex all that much, but she suspected she would be with Leonardo. Just thinking about going down on him made her quiver with anticipation. She could hardly wait. She would also insist that before he entered her he remembered to use a condom. Then, whilst she was totally protected, she would whisper for him to do *everything* to her.

A shudder ran through Veronica at this last thought. Her feelings for this man, she finally accepted, *were* dangerous. And threatening to run out of control.

Get a grip, girl, came her stern warning. *You will be going home to Australia in three weeks' time and Leonardo will become nothing but a memory. Have fun with him, like your mother said, but never forget that this will just be a fling, not a for ever moment.*

Veronica went to bed with this warning at the forefront of her mind. She fell asleep surprisingly quickly. And didn't dream. Which, when she woke, seemed a good portent for the day ahead. The weather looked excellent, the sun already up, the skies clear and cloudless. A good day for sightseeing, especially by air.

Now, what was she going to wear?

CHAPTER FIFTEEN

VERONICA DIDN'T DISOBEY Leonardo's instruction and wear a dress, despite being tempted, as she'd bought a couple of lovely sundresses for this trip. Instead, she sensibly chose three-quarter-length cuffed blue jeans, teaming them with a peasant-style pink-and-blue blouse and flat brown sandals. She gave in to vanity, however, and left her freshly shampooed hair down, hoping that her straw sunhat would control her sometimes wayward waves.

Not the only wayward thing about her, she accepted as ten o'clock approached. Despite all her warnings of the night before, her heartbeat took off and a perversely delicious tension invaded her lower body. Several deep breaths later, things hadn't improved.

Leonardo was right on time, his own outfit just as casual as her own. He too was wearing blue jeans, matched with a simple white T-shirt and lightweight navy jacket. The day might be sunny but it wasn't hot. She suspected his clothes were designer labels, because the fit and materials were superb. But she also suspected he would look just as good in anything. It was a case of the man making the clothes rather than the other way round. Leonardo was a total hunk who just exuded sex appeal. All of a sudden, Veronica wished they weren't going anywhere. She wanted to grab him and drag him inside. Wanted to spend the whole day in bed with him.

Hopefully, her eyes didn't say as much. She did have some pride left. Not a lot, she decided ruefully. But enough. Though, it wavered when he said how lovely *she* looked. Lord, but this was one wickedly seductive man.

'I'll just get the rest of my things,' she said, quickly putting her sunglasses on, then grabbing her straw bag and hat.

Locking up was achieved without any embarrassing fumbling, Veronica depositing the key in the geranium pot before glancing up at Leonardo.

'Let's hope all your wine is still there when we get back,' she quipped drily.

He grinned. 'It will be. Have you found the cellar yet?'

'No. I keep forgetting to look.'

'I'll show you where it is when we get back. This way,' he said, and cupped her left elbow, leading her not towards the stone steps but round the back of the house, where a taxi awaited them on the gravel courtyard.

It wasn't Franco's yellow convertible. This one was olive-green and much smaller. With a proper roof.

'Saturday is Franco's busiest day,' Leonardo explained as he steered her towards the already opened back door. 'This is Ricardo. Ricardo, this is Veronica, Laurence's long-lost daughter.'

Ricardo smiled at her. 'She looks like him,' he said, then just got on with the driving.

'Does everyone on Capri know who I am?' she asked quietly.

Leonardo shrugged. 'Pretty much. You can't keep any secrets on Capri. Why? Does it bother you?'

'I guess not.'

'By the way, the Hotel Fabrizzi is fully booked for tonight. With a group from America. I hate the noise, so I might have to throw myself on the mercy of one of my neighbours.'

Veronica's heart flipped over, but she managed to keep a poker face, determined not to let this devil know how excited she was by the thought of having him stay with her the whole night.

'Oh?' she said in a superbly nonchalant tone. 'Which neighbour were you thinking of asking?'

'There is only one who has a suitably large guest bedroom.'

'Will everyone on Capri know that you stayed at my place?' she asked him quietly, so that the driver couldn't hear.

'Not everyone. But *Mamma* certainly will.'

'Will that cause you problems?'

Leonardo shrugged. 'Nothing I can't handle.'

Veronica didn't doubt it.

'Let it be on your head, then, Leonardo,' she told him. 'Don't come crying to me when your parents mistakenly think your intentions towards me are serious.'

'Who says they aren't?' he asked with a look that she couldn't decipher.

It rattled her, that look. His dark eyes fairly smouldered at her from under half-lowered lids. She was still wondering what it meant when his tautly held lips split into a wide smile.

'Got you,' he said with a nudge against her ribs.

'You are a wicked man, Leonardo Fabrizzi,' she said,

both annoyed and flustered that she would think, even for a moment, that Leonardo was anything other than a highly accomplished playboy.

Leonardo grinned. 'She says I am a wicked man, Ricardo. Is she right?'

'You, Leonardo?' Ricardo threw a shocked glance over his shoulder. 'No, no. Leonardo—he is a good man. When my Louisa got sick, he pay for her to go to the best doctors in Rome. The best hospital. He always do things like that. We all love Leonardo on Capri.' And he glared at Veronica in the rear-view mirror.

'I was only joking,' she said hurriedly. 'Tell him, Leonardo.' She poked him in the ribs.

'She was only joking, Ricardo,' he reassured the taxi driver. 'She loves me too, don't you, Veronica?'

Lord, but he was incorrigible. She rolled her eyes at him. 'But of course, Leonardo. How could I not?'

'I have no idea,' he retorted, his expression one of barely controlled amusement.

Her palm itched to smack him. The man was a devil, wicked to the core. Or so she wanted to believe. But some inner instinct told Veronica that his wickedness was only skin-deep, that he had a genuinely warm heart. His love for his family and his friends spoke of a different man from the callous playboy who flitted from woman to woman, using them for his pleasure without care or commitment. Without love.

It seemed odd to her, now that she thought about it more deeply, for an Italian man of Leonardo's family background not to want to get married and have a family of his own. She wondered what it was in his past that stopped him from settling down. She doubted it was that close call with the unwanted pregnancy. Perhaps

it had something to do with his early retirement from
the sport he'd been so passionate about. She might have
asked him, if she'd imagined for a moment he would tell
her the truth. But Veronica knew instinctively that he
would not discuss his innermost feelings, certainly not
with a woman who was just a ship passing in the night.

This last thought bothered her for a few seconds,
until common sense came to the rescue. She *was* just a
ship passing in the night. That didn't mean their brief
encounter couldn't be both memorable and enjoyable.
Veronica was determined not to complicate the weekend with qualms about what she was doing with Leonardo. She was an adult. She was entitled to a sex life,
entitled to have some fun for a change. Even her mother
thought so.

So why was she feeling as though she was running a
risk in spending more time with this man? Why did the
thought of his making love to her again bring a measure of anxiety along with the inevitable excitement?
It annoyed her, this waffling in her head. *He* wasn't
worried. Just look at him sitting there, totally relaxed
in her company.

Their arrival at the helipad might have been a welcome distraction from her mental to-ing and fro-ing.
Unfortunately, the sight of the helicopter brought new
worries. She'd forgotten, for a moment, how frightened
she was of flying in one.

'Oh, dear,' she said, her stomach somersaulting as
she stared at the fragile-looking craft. It wasn't the large
one Leonardo had arrived in yesterday. This was just a
glass bubble with blades attached.

'What is it?' Leonardo asked straight away. 'What's
wrong?'

'That helicopter,' she blurted out, pointing at it as they both climbed out of the taxi. 'Is that the one we're going up in?'

'Yes. Why?'

'It looks…small.'

'It is small. It's built for just two passengers.'

She turned to stare at him with wide eyes. 'But… but…'

'Don't worry. I'm a licensed helicopter pilot. And that particular helicopter is brand new.'

CHAPTER SIXTEEN

'ARE YOU OKAY?' Leonardo asked Veronica gently as he strapped her in. She did look a little pale.

'I… I suppose so.'

'Here. Put this on,' He gave her a headset that had a microphone attached. 'Once we're up and running, it'll be noisy and you'll need this to communicate.' He showed her how to put it on before turning and putting his own on.

'Have you always been afraid of flying?' he asked, never having experienced such fear himself. He loved flying, especially when he was the pilot.

'Only in helicopters,' she told him.

'I see. Don't worry. I won't let anything happen to you.' When he leant over and touched her cheek Leonardo was surprised at how tender he felt towards her. How protective. She seemed so vulnerable all of a sudden, nothing like the rather bold creature of the night before. He would have kissed her if the microphone hadn't been in his way. Instead, he smiled over at her, catching her eye and sending her a silent message of reassurance.

Veronica's heart flipped over at the almost loving look Leonardo sent her. For a split second, she almost believed he cared about her. This was his skill as a se-ducer, she supposed. To make women think he cared.

But he didn't. Not really. She knew that. Perversely, knowing the sort of man she was dealing with made no difference to her female reaction, either to his warm smile or the promise of safety in his eyes.

'We'll start with Capri, then I'll take you over for a bird's eye view of the Amalfi coast,' he told her as she started up the engine. 'We might even fly over Mount Vesuvius.'

'But...but...' she protested, having presumed that within fifteen minutes she'd safely be back on the ground. Capri was, after all, a rather small island.

'No buts today, Veronica. I've hired this little beauty for four hours and I don't intend to waste them. After you've seen the Amalfi Coast, we'll set down at Sor-rento for lunch. I've booked us a garden table at the best *trattoria* in town. Then, if we have time, we'll fly south for a quick peek at Naples from above before heading back here. How does that sound?' he asked with a quick glance her way as they lifted off.

Veronica's stomach lifted off with them, so all Leo-nardo got in answer to his possibly rhetorical question was a sucked in gasp.

'Breathe,' he told her firmly. 'And stop worrying. I'm a very good pilot.'

She didn't doubt it. But his reassurance didn't stop her anxiety. Or the gymnastics in her stomach. His breathing advice did eventually work. Either that, or she was soon so distracted by the magnificence of the view below that she forgot to be afraid.

Leonardo circled the island three times, pointing out the same places of interest that Franco had shown her.

But everything looked better from up in the sky. Better and even more beautiful. The ancient Roman ruins. The huge rocks jutting out of the sea. The small towns and the cute little beaches. Some of the villas they flew over were splendid, with ordered gardens and big blue swimming pools, whilst others were much smaller, surrounded by different types of garden. Clearly, these houses were owned by the ordinary people who'd always lived here, not the billionaires who'd bought properties on Capri for other reasons. Privacy, perhaps. But more likely to impress. Veronica suspected there were quite a few of those.

Not Leonardo, however. Veronica was sure he didn't want to buy Laurence's villa to impress. It wasn't that kind of place. Was it just the view he coveted, or something else? She would like to ask him but not right now. Right now she didn't want to say or do anything to spoil the memory of what she was seeing.

Suddenly, the helicopter swung to the right and set off away from Capri, heading for the mainland.

'Time for the Amalfi coast now,' Leonardo said into her earphones.

She'd thought Capri was amazingly beautiful from the air, but the Amalfi coast soon showed her why it was one of the most visited tourist spots in Italy. Veronica hardly knew where to look. It was just one spectacular town after another. All of them hugged the shore with lots of the buildings perched on the very edges of breathtaking cliffs which plunged into the sea. Once again, most of the villas were white, which at the moment shone brilliantly under the midday sun.

'You like?' Leonardo said when she sighed her admiration.

'Oh, Leonardo, your country is incredible. But also a little bit scary. I wouldn't like to drive on that road down there.' And she pointed to the one that hugged the cliffs.

'You would love it, in the right car. A Ferrari would be perfect.'

'And I suppose you own a Ferrari?'

'But of course. Unfortunately, it is in Milan. I could drive it down one weekend, if you would like me to.'

'Don't be silly. I wouldn't ask you to do that. It's too far.'

He shrugged. 'The roads are good. And the car is fast.'

'I don't doubt it, with you behind the wheel. You have a thing for speed, don't you?'

'*Si*. It is a passion of mine. To do things fast. I love anything which gets my heart beating. My uncle says I am an adrenalin addict. The only time I slow down is when I'm on Capri.'

'And not always then,' she said drily.

He laughed. 'If you're referring to what happened last night, then that was more your fault then mine. When we get back to the villa I will show you how relaxed I can be in bed. Sex is one thing I don't usually rush. I like to take my time with a woman. When she lets me,' he added, casting her a rueful glance.

Veronica was thankful she wasn't a blusher, but his pointed remark evoked a blossoming of heat deep inside her. She couldn't wait for them to get back to Capri. And back to bed.

Lord, but he made her totally shameless. But then he was shameless too. She'd never met a man who spoke so openly about sex, and who just presumed she wouldn't say no.

Which of course she wouldn't. She *couldn't*. Lust

had taken possession of her body, a lust so strong and so fierce that it might have frightened her, if she hadn't been so turned on. The level of her sexual excitement propelled her past all common sense and conscience. She wanted Leonardo. And she would have him. After all, there was nothing to stop her, least of all Leonardo himself. *He* wasn't about to say no, was he?

'It's time for lunch,' he said abruptly. 'I don't know about you, but I'm suddenly very hungry.'

CHAPTER SEVENTEEN

LEONARDO DIDN'T WANT to bother with lunch. He wanted to take her straight back to Capri. It wasn't food he was hungry for. It was Veronica.

He didn't dare look at her again as he flew as fast as he could to Sorrento. That last glance had almost undone him in a way he couldn't begin to process. Because it was outside even *his* experience. Over the years he'd had countless sexual adventures with countless beautiful women. But Veronica was unlike any he'd ever encountered, a strange mixture of siren fused with the most bewitching vulnerability.

Uncharacteristically, he wanted to ask her about this man—or men—who'd hurt her in the past, but experience warned him against going down that road. Asking a girl about her emotional baggage was fraught with danger—the danger of getting emotionally involved himself. He didn't want that, especially with Veronica. Why, he wasn't sure. A reason hovered at the edge of his mind, a reason which threatened to derail him totally. So he ruthlessly pushed it aside and concentrated on what he was good at where women were concerned.

Sex.

* * *

Veronica had always been able to pick up on people's emotions by their body language. After she watched them for a while, she could see past their facade and tune into their pain, both physical and mental. It was what made her a good physio: the way she talked to her clients whilst treating them, the way she could find out what was bothering them and subtly offer some advice.

So, when Leonardo suddenly turned all stiff and silent next to her, she knew something was bothering him. But what? This time she had absolutely no idea.

They landed safely, if a little roughly, in Sorrento, a strong breeze off the sea moving the small helicopter around a bit. Strangely, Veronica had ceased to worry about surviving the flight, her focus entirely on the man beside her. She ached to say something which would break the awkward silence that had unexpectedly developed between them. Finally, just as he shut down the engine and the blades started to slow, she thought of something suitably innocuous.

'Oh, Lord, I forgot to take any photographs,' she said with true regret as she took off her headset. 'When I woke this morning to such good weather, I planned to take pictures of everything and send them to Mum.'

When he took off his own headset and smiled over at her, Veronica's heart squeezed tight with relief.

'Don't panic,' he said, his eyes holding hers. 'You can take photos on the way back, both of Sorrento and Capri.'

'You're right,' she replied, once again struck by the beauty of Leonardo's eyes. 'I can do that. No need to panic.'

But if her thudding heart was anything to go by there

was every reason to panic. She didn't want to fall in love with this man. That would be a disaster!

Keep it light and keep it sexy, she lectured herself. *Don't start worrying about what he was worrying about a minute ago. It probably wasn't anything serious, anyway. It certainly wasn't anything to do with* you.

'Gosh, we're up high here,' she said as he helped her down from the helicopter.

'Sorrento is built up on a volcanic shelf. Which reminds me. I didn't take you over Vesuvius. Sorry. I forgot.'

'That's all right. Flying over a volcano in a helicopter isn't on my bucket list.'

His eyes sparkled with genuine amusement, his earlier worries clearly gone. 'You're too young to have a bucket list.'

'Never too young for a bucket list,' she quipped back.

'Perhaps you're right.'

He took her elbow and directed her over to a waiting taxi.

'What would be on *your* bucket list?' she asked him on the way. 'If you ever made one, that is.'

'There isn't anything I want to do that I haven't tried.'

Except marriage and children, came the unexpected and unwanted thought. But then Leonardo didn't want marriage and children, did he?

Never forget that, Veronica. The man is a playboy. Which translates as a man who's stayed as a boy and who plays at life. Not a man to start having serious thoughts about. Or to care about.

'You should get your phone out and take some photos on the way to the restaurant,' he advised her. 'And again, once we're inside. This particular *trattoria* is a rather special place.'

It was. Very special. And very beautiful.

The formal dining room inside was extremely glamorous, worthy of a palace. Veronica snapped several shots of the plush surrounds and elegantly set tables. But they didn't eat there, Leonardo ushering her through to what could only be described as a garden room. It reminded Veronica of eating under the pergola last night. But this was on a much grander scale, with glass and iron-work tables instead of wood, and the plushest of cushions on the chairs. Above, across an intricate framework hung a canopy, not of grape vines, but an assortment of climbing vines which boasted scented flowers of all colours. The sky could be glimpsed through the odd break in the foliage, suggesting that this room would be unavailable if it was raining.

But it wasn't raining. The day was glorious, as was the setting, the service *and* the company.

'What would you like to drink?' Leonardo asked as he perused the drinks menu. 'I won't be having any alcohol myself. I never drink when I'm flying. I'll just be having mineral water.'

'Then I will too,' she said, not wanting to be tempted to get herself tipsy to soothe her nerves. If she was going to have a fling with Leonardo—which undoubtedly she was—then she preferred to do it with a clear head.

'Are you sure?' he asked. 'You don't even want one glass of wine?'

'No, your company is intoxicating enough,' she quipped flirtatiously.

Surprise flashed into his eyes for a split second, followed by a wry smile.

'You don't have to flatter me, Veronica,' he said. 'I'm a sure thing.'

She couldn't help it. She laughed.

'I'm so glad to hear that, Leonardo,' Veronica said, deciding this was the way to play it—light-heartedly and a bit naughtily. 'Last night was over far too quickly.'

'I fully agree. It was little more than an entree. But, speaking of food, here comes the waiter. Would you like me to order for you?'

'Si,' she said, and he grinned at her.

Veronica had no idea what he ordered but felt confident it would all be delicious.

The mineral water arrived quickly, as did a small plate of herbed bread.

'Would you mind if I asked you something personal?' she said once the waiter departed.

'That depends,' came his careful answer. 'I told you before, I don't discuss past relationships.'

Her smile was amused. 'You don't *have* any past relationships to discuss, from what I've read. No, I'm curious about why you want to buy the villa so much. Is it just the view, or somewhere private to escape to when you visit your parents?'

'I suppose it's a bit of both. But it also holds good memories for me. The weeks I stayed with Laurence after I broke my ankle were some of the happiest in my life. I learned to control my usual restless self and found pleasure in activities other than the physical. Of course, I have your father to thank for that. He was a man of the mind more than the body. And a very good teacher.'

Veronica found it hard not to feel jealous. How she would love to have spent weeks at the villa with her father; to be taught chess by him, and listen to his favourite music sitting by his side on the terrace. She might have even learned to appreciate wine.

Still, it was good to hear nice things about him, even if it was second-hand information.

'How did you break your ankle?' she asked. 'Skiing, I suppose.'

'No. Rock climbing.'

'Oh, Lord, you are a one, aren't you?'

He shrugged. 'I can't help it. I like physical challenges.'

'Perhaps you should stick to less risky ones.'

'Like making love all night, perhaps?'

Their eyes locked, Veronica seeing the sizzling hunger in his, *knowing* that her own eyes were just as hungry.

It was fortuitous that the entree arrived at that moment, a steaming pasta dish with bacon, aubergine and mushroom. Veronica welcomed the opportunity to look away from Leonardo's hot gaze.

'This is delicious,' she said after a couple of mouthfuls. 'Glad it's just a small serving, though. It's rather filling.'

'That's why I ordered grilled swordfish for the main, with just a light salad. I wanted to leave some room for dessert.'

Veronica winced. 'I hope it's not as fattening as that dessert your mother served me last night.'

'Not quite.'

When it finally arrived, Veronica gave him a droll look.

'You are such a liar,' she said as she eyed the large custard-filled pastry served with a huge dollop of whipped cream. But it was too mouth-watering to resist. Just like Leonardo.

'I thought you might need some extra calories to survive the night ahead,' he drawled.

Veronica tried to think of a witty comeback but she couldn't, her mind having gone blank at his provocative remark.

The dessert was followed by coffee which would have brought Lazarus back from the dead, and which left Veronica feeling quite hyped up. But underneath the caffeine-induced buzz lay some very female nerves. Silly, really, given she'd loved their passionate encounter last night.

But this was different, wasn't it? Last night had been brilliant but spontaneous. To *plan* sex, to anticipate it as she had done all day, was not conducive to calm. It was like sitting an important exam. No matter how many times you'd done exams before, no matter how much you'd studied the subject, there was always that fear of something cropping up that would throw you.

Best leave everything up to him, Veronica determined as he paid the bill then steered her out to another waiting taxi. *He obviously knows what to do. He's had enough practice.*

The flight back to Capri was still a welcome distraction, Veronica taking photographs of absolutely everything.

'Mum's going to want to come here for a holiday after I send her these,' she said at one point.

'Then she should,' Leonardo replied. 'She can stay at the villa.'

'It'll be *your* villa soon.'

'True.'

'She could stay at the Hotel Fabrizzi,' Veronica said with a mischievous glance. 'I can recommend it.'

'Would you come with her?'

'Probably. But if I did we wouldn't stay at your parents' hotel. Sophia might think I'd come back to see you and start matchmaking again.'

When he just shrugged at that, she shook her head at him. 'You really shouldn't encourage her, you know. She honestly thinks you're in the market for a wife.'

'I've found that to argue with *Mamma* only encourages her more. Besides, I *will* be in the market for a wife. One day. When the right girl comes along,' he added in a drily amused voice.

She snorted at that. 'Your *mamma* will be long gone by then. You are a cruel man, Leonardo.'

'Not at all,' he denied. 'I am a very kind man. But at the moment I'm also a very single man. And enjoying it,' he added with the wickedest glance thrown her way.

A sexually charged shiver rippled down her spine, heat spreading through her lower body. Her nipples hardened and her belly tightened. All from just a look.

Oh, my.

'Go back to taking your photographs, Veronica,' he ordered thickly. 'And I'll go back to making sure we get down safely. There's a strong wind blowing over Capri and this is a very light machine.'

He got them down safely, but he was right about the wind. It whipped her hair into a right mess on the way to the waiting taxi, which thankfully wasn't Franco's. No way did she want to make idle conversation with Franco who, she suspected, was somewhat of a gossip.

Finger-combing her hair into some semblance of order, she climbed into the taxi ahead of Leonardo, who told the driver to take them to the Hotel Fabrizzi.

She winced at this, not wanting to endure talking to *any* of Leonardo's family, especially not his mother.

'It's all right,' he whispered to her. '*Mamma* will be busy inside. You can dash off up the path to the villa and I'll follow shortly. I just have to collect a few things for my overnight stay.'

'But what will they all think?' she whispered back.

He shrugged again, that dismissive shrug he used a lot. 'I refuse to live my life by other people's expectations. Now, hush up.'

She fell silent then. And so did he.

It was only a short drive from the helipad to the hotel. But the silence made it seem longer. It was so sexy, that silence, sending Veronica's head spinning with desire. By the time they turned into the courtyard she was agitated beyond belief. She hurried out of the taxi then rushed away from him, under the pergola and up the steep steps. She didn't look back. She knew he would soon come after her; knew they would soon be together.

Another erotic shiver raced through her as she dived into the pot to retrieve the front-door key. No, not a shiver this time. A shudder. The kind of bone-shaking shudder that a floundering ship might make. It reminded Veronica of her earlier idea that she and Leonardo were ships passing in the night.

If only that were true…

They weren't ships passing in the night, without consequences or complications. They were on a collision course.

Veronica shuddered again as she ran inside. She was still nervous but not afraid. She should have been afraid. Why wasn't she afraid? Why was it that she didn't care about consequences or complications? Was this what lust did to you—made you reckless and foolish? Made you uncaring of anything but the promise of pleasure?

Not that Leonardo was a promise of pleasure. He *was* pleasure.

Such thinking made Veronica feel hot and sticky all over. She winced at the thought that she might smell of perspiration. And other things…

She'd always been very particular about personal hygiene, hating it when clients came to her without having a shower first. Would she have time for a quick shower? she wondered.

It had only been a minute since she'd left Leonardo. Surely it would be at least another five minutes before he made an appearance? His mother was likely to collar him and ask him innumerable questions about their day together.

Veronica was already stripping as she hurried towards the master bedroom with its lovely *en suite* bathroom.

CHAPTER EIGHTEEN

LEONARDO WAS GRATEFUL that the hotel was rather chaotic inside, with guests coming and going. He was able to slip into his room and get what he needed for the night without being accosted by his mother or father. Elena did grab him on the way out from where she was stationed behind Reception.

'Going somewhere?' she asked in Italian after eyeing his overnight bag.

'I'm staying in Laurence's guest room tonight,' he replied, also in Italian. 'I can't stand the noise when this place is full.'

'Veronica doesn't mind?' his sister asked with a knowing glint in her eye.

'Why should she mind? She came here to find out about her father. I had more to do with Laurence than any of you so I can tell her everything she wants to know.'

Elena smiled. 'She's very beautiful. She's also very nice. She would make some lucky man a good wife.'

He just smiled, told her not to meddle and left.

But his smile didn't last for long.

It annoyed him lately, how much his family were trying to press him into settling down. He had no intention of marrying some poor girl just to secure an heir. Who cared about carrying on bloodlines and family names these days? It was archaic.

Leonardo hurried as he headed for the path which led up to the villa.

Still…it probably *was* a mistake to stay the whole night with Veronica. He'd always kept his sex life away from Capri. He'd never brought a girlfriend to his parents' hotel, knowing that it was a bad idea. He came here to relax, not get himself into a total twist. Laurence's villa used to be his sanctuary, his refuge. When he'd sat on the terrace, soaking in the view and sipping some of Laurence's fine wine, all his inner demons used to slip away. He hadn't thought about that awful time when the true love of his life—competitive skiing—had been snatched away. He hadn't paced around like he did in his office. He hadn't needed sex to distract him. He'd actually relaxed.

He wasn't relaxed now, was he?

Hell, no. That witch of a girl had undone him, big time.

Leonardo charged up the stone steps two at a time, lust making him impatient.

The sliding glass door being open made him laugh. *Not too worried about security now, eh, Veronica?* Her mind was obviously on other things. He'd felt the sexual tension in her in the taxi. Seen the desire in her dilated eyes.

She wouldn't need much foreplay the first time, he decided as he walked in, dumped his bag in the guest room then went to look for her. The whole day had been foreplay.

When he heard the shower running, Leonardo strode purposefully in its direction.

He'd never actually been in Laurence's bedroom before. But it was a mirror image of the guest bedroom at the other end of the house, just with different furnishings. The bathroom was exactly the same too, the floor and walls covered in grey-and-white marble tiles.

Veronica was in the shower. Naked, of course, her nudity obscured slightly by the glass screen. Even so, he stared.

He hadn't seen her naked before. God, but she was lovely. He adored every inch of her slender but very feminine figure. She had just enough breast. Just enough everything. Leonardo had never been attracted to voluptuous women. He preferred athletic-looking girls.

She must have sensed him standing there in the doorway, staring at her, because suddenly her head whipped round and their eyes met through the wet glass. Did she blush, or was it the heat of the water making her cheeks pink?

When he stepped forward and slid back the screen, she snapped off the taps, then spun round to face him, nervously touching her hair that she'd bundled up on top of her head.

'I… I didn't think you'd be this quick,' she said shakily. 'And I was hot.'

That she was, he thought. But he wasn't crass enough to say so. Instead, he handed her one of the two white towels hanging nearby. She grabbed it and wrapped it around her dripping body, her eyes still touchingly vulnerable. Surely she couldn't be shy? She certainly hadn't been last night.

'I might have a quick shower myself,' he said. 'I could do with cooling down a bit.'

And wasn't that the truth. Leonardo already planned to make it an icy cold shower. The last thing he wanted was a repeat of last night's performance. He'd acted like some randy school boy, unable to control himself.

'Why don't you get us both a couple of glasses of wine?' he suggested. 'And I'll be with you ASAP.'

'Oh. Oh, all right. Does it matter what wine?'

'No. Whatever Carmelina put in the fridge is okay with me.'

Veronica tried not to think as she went in search of the wine; tried not to feel embarrassed at his catching her in the shower. After all, *he* wasn't embarrassed. She suspected that *nothing* embarrassed him. Certainly not nudity.

There were several bottles of white wine in the door of the fridge. Veronica selected a Chablis, then searched the kitchen cupboards for glasses. There were lots, especially wine glasses. One set attracted her. They were quite large, but with long, fine stems in a beautiful shade of green glass. Was it her father who'd liked green glass? she wondered. Or his wife?

This last thought reminded Veronica how quickly she'd been distracted from her quest to find out everything she could about her father. It was all Leonardo's fault, she decided when he walked in, obviously naked beneath the white towel draped low around his hips.

Lord, but he was just so beautiful; the most beautiful man she'd ever seen. She couldn't think of any model or movie star who could compare. He was just so perfect. His face. His skin. His body.

It was his body she kept staring at now. She'd become rather used to his handsome face and his lovely olive skin. But she wasn't used to seeing this much of his gorgeous body. Last night was just a blur in her mind. Over far too quickly. Her heart pounded as her eyes travelled over him from head to toe.

Talk about every woman's fantasy come true!

Veronica had always been attracted to fit men. Not the muscle-bound, weight-lifting type. She preferred the runners and the rowers, men with flab-free stomachs and long, strong legs. Leonardo had all that and more. His shape was perfection in her eyes, from his naturally broad shoulders to his flat stomach, his small waist and slim hips anchored by long, sexy legs.

Her hand surprised her when it didn't shake as she handed him a glass of wine.

He took it and lifted it to his lips, his eyes never leaving hers over the rim. The air in the room suddenly felt thick with a tension which she knew could only be eased one way. But she stayed exactly where she was, lifting her own glass and taking a deep swallow. Not that she needed any alcohol to make her body zing. Every nerve-ending she owned was already electrified.

He drank the whole glass with agonising slowness, all the while just looking at her. Not at her body, but deep, deep into her eyes, searching for a sign perhaps that he could proceed. Either that, or he was just cruelly making her wait.

Finally, just when the anticipation became almost unbearable, Leonardo put his glass down on the nearby counter and closed the gap between them. A slow smile curved his mouth as he took her glass out of her hands and placed it next to his. When he turned back she thought he was going to kiss her. But he didn't. Instead, he reached up and pulled her hair down from the loose knot into which she'd wound it before her shower. It tumbled down around her naked shoulders, thick, soft and wavy. Her crowning glory, her mother always said.

'I've been wanting to do this all day,' he murmured as he ran his fingers through her hair.

Veronica blinked. 'But my hair was down all day.'

'I meant I wanted to touch it.'

'Oh…'

'And to touch *you*.' His hands left her hair and trailed down the sides of her throat then moved under her hair to her shoulders. He cupped them gently, then pulled her close, his mouth descending to hers as though in slow motion. Her own arms hung limply at her sides whilst her head grew light with the most dizzying waves of desire. Despite her seeming attitude of submission, her lips were already parted by the time his made contact, his low groan showing her that he was as turned on as she was. But still he didn't hurry, his tongue sliding sinuously into her mouth until she was beside herself with longing and need.

Her moan betrayed the extent of that need. Leonardo's head immediately lifted.

'*Si,*' he rasped. 'It is torture, is it not?'

She didn't answer him. She *couldn't*.

'You deserve to be tortured,' he ground out as he suddenly bent to scoop her up into his arms. 'You are the sort of woman who drives men mad, with your big violet eyes and your flirtatious ways.'

Veronica found her tongue as he carried her back to the master bedroom. 'I think you've got that the wrong way round, Leonardo. *You* are the sort of man who drives *women* mad. And you know it.'

He looked shocked for a second, and then he shrugged. 'I do have a good record with the ladies.'

Veronica couldn't help it. She started to giggle, and then she really started to laugh.

He threw her onto the bed as he had the night before, his hands finding his hips as he glared down at her.

'I don't see what you find so funny,' he growled.

'Don't you?' She stopped laughing but the corners of her mouth kept itching to smile. He, however, remained standing there with his legs apart, his hands clamped to his hips and his eyes all narrowed and angry. Talk about a typical Italian male! They really didn't have a great sense of humour. But she liked them all the same with their proud, passionate ways.

'I thought we were going to have sex, Leonardo,' she said. 'Not argue.'

His sensually carved lips pouted in the most deliciously sexy way.

'I do not want to have sex with you, Veronica,' he said in clipped tones.

Her eyes widened, her dismay acute. 'You don't?'

'No. I don't. We did that last night. Today, I want to make love to you.'

Her heart flipped right over. Okay, so they were only words, but they were lovely words. *Loving* words. It had been so long since she'd heard loving words said to her. Too long, perhaps. Leonardo's words touched the very depths of her soul.

Be careful here, Veronica, came the protective warning. *Be very careful.*

'I'd like that,' she said, trying not to sound too needy.

'Good.' His face softened as he reached down and plucked the towel away from her. But his eyes stayed hot. Hot and hungry.

'Bellissima,' he murmured, then tossed his own towel away.

He was the one who was *bellissimo*, Veronica thought, looking away from his stunning erection as she wriggled herself around on the bed so that the back of her head rested on the pillows. Leonardo climbed onto the bed, stretching out next to her. He propped himself up on his left elbow whilst he caressed her with his right hand, first one breast and then the other, his gaze intent on the reactions of her nipples, which tightened under his touch.

When she made a small gasp of pleasure, his eyes lifted to hers. 'You like that, don't you?' he said, smiling softly.

'Yes,' she choked out.

'What about this?' he asked, taking the nipple furthest from him between his thumb and forefinger, and slowly but firmly starting to squeeze.

'Oh, God!' she cried out as an electrifying shard of sensation rocketed through her body, making her belly tighten and her thighs quiver.

'And this?' he went on, holding the nipple with a hard grip and twisting it from right to left.

She moaned. It was not a moan of protest or pain. But it wasn't pleasure, either. This wasn't making love, she thought wildly. This was something else, something dark, delicious and troubling. Troubling because she liked it *too* much.

'No, don't,' she half-sobbed after he kept doing it. 'Don't.'

To give him credit he stopped straight away. 'I didn't mean to hurt you,' he said, his expression remorseful.

'Just kiss me,' she said shakily.

He did. And it was lovely. She wrapped her arms around him and drew him down on top of her. Soon, the kissing wasn't enough, of course. Dear heaven, but she wanted him so much. Her legs moved out from under him, spreading wide, her knees lifting in blatant invitation. He groaned, then obliged, sliding into her after only a momentary hesitation. It was fantastic, the feel of his flesh filling hers, the way he rocked back and forth inside her. Her hips moved with him, urging him deeper and deeper. He groaned again, the sound one of torment and frustration. When his rhythm picked up, the sensations were mind-blowing. She'd never felt such pleasure. Or such tension. She was panting and praying, wanting to come but not wanting it to end.

'Dio,' he growled, then came, his violent ejaculation propelling her into an orgasm that was as powerful as it was primal. Her fingernails dug into his back as her body bucked under his. Her mind was just as splintered, uncaring of anything but the ecstasy of the here and now.

CHAPTER NINETEEN

LEONARD COULDN'T BELIEVE he'd done it again. He'd lost control and not used a condom. Yet he'd put a couple on the bedside chest earlier, along with his phone and his watch.

Not that it mattered, he supposed.

Or did it? Could he really trust that Veronica was on the pill, like she'd said?

He withdrew abruptly, rolling away from her with a worried sigh.

'What is it?' she asked straight away. 'What's wrong?'

'Nothing,' he muttered, angry with himself now. 'Just…' He glanced over at her, not wanting to spoil things between them, but he simply had to say something. 'I didn't use a condom again.'

'Oh,' she said, blinking as though she herself had only just realised. 'I meant to ask you to use one. But I forgot.'

'I guess it doesn't matter, since you're on the pill,' he went on. 'But let's face it, even the pill isn't one hundred percent safe.'

Now it was her turn to sigh. 'True.'

He wished he hadn't brought the matter up. What they'd just shared had been incredible and he hated that he might have ruined the chance of more of the same.

'Look, Leonardo,' she said with an edge to her voice. 'Trust me when I say there's nothing for you to worry about. Aside from anything else, my period is due on Monday. If by some perverse twist of fate the worst happened, then I would handle it. I certainly wouldn't use a baby to trap you into marriage.'

He couldn't help being shocked. 'You'd have a termination?' He didn't believe in abortion; he had been brought up to think of all life as sacred.

'I didn't say that,' she snapped, sitting up and swinging her legs over the side of the bed. 'I need to go to the bathroom.'

Veronica just made it onto the toilet before the tears came. She didn't know why she was so upset. Perhaps because one minute she'd been lying underneath Leonardo's utterly gorgeous body, thinking she'd died and gone to heaven, and the next he'd rolled away from her, leaving her feeling both abandoned and unloved. He'd spoiled her little romantic fantasy with his worries about having unsafe sex.

It did bother her a bit that once again she herself hadn't thought of protection, especially after she'd planned to insist on it this time. But of course at the back of her mind she'd known she was ninety-nine percent safe. Did he honestly think she'd deliberately risk falling pregnant to a man like him?

The very thought appalled her. At the same time, it upset her that he would think she was anything like that other girl who'd lied to him so shamefully.

But you lied to him too, Veronica. By omission. You let him think you're on the pill but you aren't. Just be-

cause you know it's the wrong time of the month to conceive is not an excuse. You still lied to him.

Guilt had her biting her bottom lip. As did regret. The trouble was it was too late to tell him the truth now. He was a cynical man, and possibly ignorant of how well a woman could know her own body. He wouldn't understand that there really was very little risk. She was as regular as clockwork. The only time in years when it had been disrupted was when Jerome had died. Shock and stress, the doctor had said. But eventually everything had settled back into its normal rhythm, not missing a beat since.

Veronica sighed then stood up. Whilst washing her hands, a quick glance in the vanity mirror showed a tear-stained face and very messy hair. Without stopping to think, she dived into the shower again, turning on the taps, squealing when it came out freezing cold at first. She squealed again when Leonardo suddenly pulled back the screen door.

'Are you all right?' he asked anxiously.

'The…the water was c-cold,' she stammered. 'It…it's getting warmer now.'

His frown smoothed out, replaced by an apologetic smile. 'I am a fool,' he said. 'I trust you, Veronica. Truly I do. Forgive me?'

He didn't wait for a reply, stepping into the shower with her and pulling her into his arms. They kissed under the warm jets of water. Then kissed some more. Leonardo ran his hands up and down her back, then stayed down, cupping her buttocks and yanking her hard against him. His head lifted then and he laughed. 'See what you do to me? Anyone would think I hadn't had sex in months.'

'Poor Leonardo. How long has it been, then?' she asked him with a coquettish glance. 'A whole week at least?'

'Longer than that,' he protested.

'*Two* weeks?'

'You really do have a bad opinion of me. Let me assure you that, since Laurence passed away, sex has been the last thing on my mind.'

His mentioning her father made Veronica sigh. 'I came here to find out about my father, and all I've wanted to do since I arrived so far is be with you. You're like a drug, Leonardo. A very addictive drug.'

'Is that a criticism or a compliment?'

'I'm sure you'll take it as a compliment.'

'If you insist,' he said. And he grinned down at her. 'Come. I'm not one for making love in showers. I much prefer the comfort of a bed.' So saying, he leant past her and turned off the taps before pushing open the glass door. The nearest towel rail was empty, however, both towels still on the bedroom floor where Leonardo had dropped them.

'There are more towels in the utility room,' Veronica informed him—not very helpfully, since the utility room was some distance away.

'I think we'll just make a dash for the bedroom. Use the towels we left there.'

'All right,' she said, wringing out her hair so that it wouldn't drip too much.

They were like two naughty teenagers who'd gone skinny dipping in the sea and had to run for their clothes. They both made a dive for the nearest towel, actually having a mock tug-of-war before Leonardo gave in and let her have it. She didn't wrap it around herself this time, just rubbed herself dry then bent forward and wound it around her wet hair, before straightening and scrambling into the bed, where she sat up against the pillows with her arms crossed over her bare breasts and her turbaned head feeling ridiculously heavy.

'All done,' she said.

Leonardo shook his own head at her. 'No way,' he said. 'I'm not making love to you with a towel on your head. Take it off.'

There was something in his eyes which put paid to the momentary temptation to refuse. Leonardo, when crossed, was nothing like his usual smiling, charming self. His whole face darkened, his shoulders stiffened. No wonder he'd been such a fierce competitor on the ski slopes. He didn't like to lose. And he didn't like a woman to say no to him.

'My hair's still wet,' she complained, even as she removed the towel and tossed it away.

'I like you wet,' he replied, his good humour restored. As was his sexually charged persona.

Veronica tried to find something saucy to say back but he'd already climbed into the bed beside her, and then he pulled her down under him.

'None of this, either,' he said as he took hold of her arms and placed them up above her head on the pillows. He didn't hold them there, thank God. She would not have liked that. Or maybe she would have. She seemed to like everything he did to her. She certainly liked it when he slid down her body and started making love to her with his mouth. She loved it, just as she'd imagined she would. He knew exactly where to kiss and where to lick. His lips and tongue were knowing enough, aided adeptly by hands which knew how to move and lift her to give that questing mouth better access to all of her.

He shocked her at times, but she never wanted him to stop. The only sounds coming from her open, panting mouth were the gasps and groans whenever she came: three times in as many minutes. She could hardly believe it. Multiple orgasms were unknown to her personally. She'd heard of them but thought they existed only in books and the imagination of fiction writers.

Not so. This was real. This was her, about to come again.

This time, Leonardo stopped just in time, sliding up her body and into her, taking her breath away with the size of his erection. Clearly, doing what he'd been doing had been a huge turn-on for him as well.

She expected to come straight away but, strangely, she didn't. Maybe she'd run out of orgasms for the day. But slowly, and quite deliciously, his steady rhythm stoked the fire back into her. Her hips began to move with him. He groaned, then whispered her name with the kind of warmth and passion that she'd never heard on any man's lips. Certainly not Jerome's. His lovemaking, whilst skilful, had been on the clinical side.

Suddenly, something broke within her. Something she could not identify. Not a physical thing but something deeply emotional, evoking a sense of bonding which compelled her to take her arms down from the pillow and wind them tightly around him.

'Leonardo,' she whispered back.

Only then did she come. And so did he, their bodies surrendering, not in a clash of wild shuddering but in gently rolling spasms which made Veronica want to cry. She did cry. But silently. The spasms seemed to go on for ever, which was just as well, giving her tears time to dry and for some common sense to return.

I have not fallen in love with Leonardo, she told herself sternly. *He's just very good at this. Very, very good. Get a grip, Veronica.*

She might have got a grip if she'd had time. And if she wasn't so exhausted. But sleep beckoned, a dark curtain having already fallen over her mind. Her body soon followed. She didn't see Leonardo frown down at her as he withdrew. She couldn't worry about his body language, which spoke of concern and confusion.

Leonardo lay beside her, unable to sleep, which was unusual for him after so much sex. He was troubled. The thought that he liked Veronica too much troubled him. Way too much.

Because let's face it, Leonardo, he thought to himself, *what you felt when you made love to Veronica just now far surpassed anything you've ever felt before.* It had been more than sex. It had felt suspiciously like what he'd imagined falling in love would be like.

The problem was he didn't want to fall in love with Veronica. He didn't want to fall in love with *any* woman just yet but, if it had to happen, he certainly didn't want it to happen with a twenty-eight-year-old Australian girl who carried way too much emotional baggage and who obviously believed he was some kind of man whore.

He wasn't. Not in *his* book. Okay, so his girlfriends didn't last very long. They bored him after a while, as did many aspects of life nowadays. But he only ever had one girlfriend at a time, and not nearly as many as social media suggested. He didn't cheat on them. Never. He always broke up with them before entering another relationship. Yes, he did have the occasional one-night stand. But only when he was between girlfriends, and only when he was in one of his dark, restless moods.

Leonardo could feel one of those dark moods descending right now. God, but he hated it when he felt like this. So out of control. He'd been out of bloody control ever since he'd met the girl beside him, who was sleeping like a baby with not a worry in the world. Damn her with her violet eyes and her oh, so kissable mouth. And damn Laurence for leaving his villa to her.

Laurence...

If only Laurence were still alive. He'd used to be able to get Leonardo out of his black moods. He'd put on some classical music, pour him some wine and they'd sit on the terrace, if it was summer, or by the fireplace in winter, not always talking, sometimes just listening and drinking. Relaxing.

He supposed he could get up and do that now. But it wouldn't be the same, doing any of that by himself. It wouldn't work, either. He needed Laurence's logical reasoning and pragmatic presence to do the trick. He'd had a way about him, that man. If Leonardo were honest, Veronica had a similar way. She was great company and very easy to talk to. He'd thoroughly enjoyed their sightseeing trip this morning. And their lunch in Sorrento. Unfortunately, the sexual chemistry flaring between them was difficult to ignore, bringing an irritation which he'd struggled to control.

That was what bothered him almost as much as possibly falling in love—his lack of control. Though maybe they were both wrapped up in the same package. He still could not get over not having used protection. What on earth had he been thinking?

But it was done now. And truthfully, it had felt fantastic. Was that what was tricking him, his level of physical pleasure? The sheer intimacy of it all?

Possibly. He liked that thought. It made sense. He probably wasn't falling in love with her at all. He was just blown away by how great it felt without using a condom. It was many years, after all, since he'd had the pleasure of spontaneous sex. He'd liked that there'd been no need to turn away and risk spoiling the moment. No matter how quick you were, that was sometimes very annoying.

A yawn captured him. Maybe he could sleep now that he'd worked out his emotions.

Leonardo rolled over and put an arm around Veronica. She snuggled back into him till they were like two spoons fitted together. Leonardo smiled with contentment, then fell fast sleep, happy with the thought that she would be there for him when he awoke.

CHAPTER TWENTY

SHE WASN'T.

Leonardo's eyes opened to an empty space next to him. He stretched, wondering what time it was and how long Veronica had been up. The blinds in the bedroom weren't down, and he could see that it wasn't yet night. Reaching for his phone, he checked the time. Not that late. Only six-thirty, and daylight saving meant it would be light for some time yet.

Rising, Leonardo headed for the bathroom where he'd dropped his clothes. Five minutes later, he left the bedroom in search of Veronica. He found her sitting at Laurence's desk, which was tucked away in an alcove in a corner of the living room. She was dressed too, a mug of steaming coffee at her elbow, her eyes fixed on the computer in front of her.

Laurence's computer.

'There you are,' he said, and she swung round in the chair to face him.

God, but she was beautiful, he thought. Even without make-up and with her hair up.

'I didn't want to wake you,' she said coolly, and picked up her coffee, 'So I had a shower in the guest room and got dressed there. I've been trying to get into my father's computer, but it's password protected.'

'I know the password,' he offered.

'You do?' She blinked up at him in surprise.

'He gave it to me when I was staying here with my broken ankle. I couldn't sleep some nights so I would get up and play poker on the computer. What are you hoping to find?' he asked as he came over and tapped in the password, which wasn't exactly obscure. Just Ruth with her birthdate after it. Of course, he had to lean over her shoulder to do that, his nostrils immediately assailed with a faint but tantalising scent. Not perfume. Possibly just shower gel.

'Anything, really,' she said, and quickly stood up. 'Would you like some coffee?'

'Si. Grazie.'

'Why are you speaking Italian all of sudden?' she demanded to know.

He shrugged. 'Does it matter?'

'No. Yes. I mean, I understand a few words, but I'd prefer you to use English.'

'Fine.' He smiled at her then sat down in front of the computer. 'Let's see if I can find anything enlightening for you.' He brought up Laurence's email account and tapped in the same password, guessing that it would be the same.

It was. Of course, there was a whole heap of spam, sent after Laurence's demise. He deleted it all then back-tracked to the days before Laurence had left for London. One email jumped out at him. It was from a private investigation firm in Sydney and was accompanied by a PDF. Leonardo downloaded it, frowning as he began to read, his frown deepening by the time he'd read the report, which wasn't overly long, but which included an attached photograph.

'I remembered from lunch that you liked your coffee black and strong,' Veronica said as she set a steaming mug down on the desk next to him. 'Have you found something?'

Had he found something? *Dio*, had he ever!

Veronica peered over Leonardo's shoulder at the computer screen.

'My God,' she gasped, pointing at the screen. 'That's me.'

'That it is,' Leonardo said slowly.

'But…but…'

'It's attached to a recent report from a private detective agency based in Sydney,' he explained. 'Clearly Laurence wanted to find out how you were faring before he died. Also clearly,' he added, glancing up into her widening eyes, 'What he discovered made him decide to change his will and leave you his villa here on Capri.'

'What…what does it say about me?' she asked, obviously shaken by this news.

And well she should be, Leonardo thought, not sure if he felt sad for her. Or furious that she had deceived him.

'I think it best that I print out the report and let you read it for yourself,' he said with creditable composure.

'All right,' she agreed.

'Perhaps you should also sit down.'

Veronica sank onto the nearest dining room chair, her heart sinking as well. She knew exactly what the report would say, her mind scrambling to find some ex-

cuse she could give to Leonardo as to why she'd let
him think she'd been out there, socialising and having
an active sex life, one that required her to take the pill.
Oh, Lord! She had to keep that lie going. Leonardo
would be understandably furious if she told him she
wasn't on the pill.

Her stomach tightened as the printer spat out the
report.

She wondered if the investigator had found out the
whole truth about Jerome as well.

Possibly not. He'd hidden his affair well.

'Here,' Leonardo said, and slapped the pages down
on the dining table. He was angry with her, she could
see. Which was understandable.

The report wasn't long. Only three pages. But it
spelled the situation out exactly as she'd feared. It
made her sound like some grieving widow, not the bitter wronged woman she actually was. Or had been.

But she wasn't that woman any longer, was she?
Leonardo had shown her she'd been a fool to hide away,
nursing her grievances and shunning the opposite sex.
Okay, so he wasn't the kind of man to pin any future
hopes on. Which was bad luck. She did so like him.
But he'd still been good for her, giving her back her li-
bido, along with a more optimistic way of looking at
the opposite sex. She would remember him for the rest
of her life.

Veronica decided then and there to embrace the truth.
Though, not as far as Jerome's affair. Leonardo had
already said he didn't want to hear any man-bashing.
And, really, it was none of his business. Neither would
she be telling him she wasn't on the pill.

'Well?' Leonardo prompted, having drawn out a

chair opposite her and sat down. 'What have you got to say for yourself?'

Veronica's lifted her eyebrows in a nonchalant gesture. 'There's not much I can say. The report has spelt it out and it's all true. My fiancé was killed in a motorcycle accident just before our wedding. I was devastated, then deeply depressed for a long time. And, yes, ever since then I've lived the life of a nun. There haven't been any sheikhs or any other men in my life, or in my bed, for three years.'

'Not exactly the impression you gave me, is it?' he threw at her.

Her shrug was a brilliant echo of the shrugs he often used. 'What can I say? When I found out Laurence was my father and that he'd left me a villa on Capri, I finally saw the error of my ways. I decided then and there to throw off my nun's habit and start living life again.'

His lips pursed, his dark eyes narrowing with obvious distrust.

'So when did you start taking the pill?' he demanded to know.

'Girls take the pill these days for many reasons,' Veronica said haughtily, but with her fingers crossed under the table. 'It protects you from osteoporosis, as well as reducing premenstrual tension. It is not always about avoiding an unwanted pregnancy, although nothing beats a condom for safe sex,' she added tartly for good measure.

The best defence was always attack. Or so she'd read.

He looked both distracted and offended. 'You keep on saying things like that,' he snapped. 'I assure you, I am perfectly safe. And I am not as bad as you think.'

'Yes you are, Leonardo. But no sweat. I like you the

way you are. You're great fun, and fantastic in bed. On top of that, I certainly won't have to worry about leaving you behind with a broken heart when I go back to Australia.'

His mouth opened then closed like a floundering fish's.

She might have laughed if her last words hadn't made her own heart lurch all of a sudden. Maybe *she* was the one who should worry about going back with a broken heart.

Leonardo finally found his tongue. 'I don't know what to say,' he said, sounding totally flummoxed.

'You don't have to say anything, do you?'

CHAPTER TWENTY-ONE

LEONARDO TRIED TO keep his outrage going, but it was hard in the face of her nonchalance over the situation. When she smiled at him, he simply had to smile back.

'Truly,' he said with a shake of his head. 'You are impossible!'

'So my mother tells me. Oh, Lord, that reminds me,' she said, jumping up and leaving the report on the dining table.

'Where are you going?'

'To get my phone and send Mum the photos I took today. I might ring her as well. You go drink your coffee and see if you can find anything more on that computer. Then afterwards you can show me where the wine cellar is. I also might have to rustle up something for us to eat. I don't know how late it is, but I'm starting to feel darned hungry.'

She dashed off, leaving Leonardo staring after her with hunger of a different kind.

Shaking his head at himself, he reached over and picked up the report, reading it through again. Nothing new struck him, though this time he felt more compassion for Veronica's plight. It must have been very hard for her, losing the man she loved shortly before their wedding. The first time he'd read the report his reaction had been shock, plus anger at the way she'd deceived him. Leonardo was never good with female deception. Now, admiration crept in with his compassion. It had been brave of her to throw off her depression and come to Capri. Brave to adopt a brighter, happier personality, instead of the dreary one which came across in that report.

Laurence had done a good thing, leaving her this place. Though, damn it all, he should have contacted his daughter earlier. She was his flesh and blood. Okay, so she might not have been conceived in the normal way, but what did that matter? She was still family.

When Leonardo folded the pages over then stood up, a memory teased his mind, a memory of Laurence doing exactly the same thing that last weekend. Clearly, he'd been reading this very report when Leonardo had come to visit him. But, also clearly, Laurence hadn't wanted to tell him about it. Instead, he'd folded the pages and hurried away, hiding the contents from him. Why? Leonardo was puzzled. They'd been very close friends. With Ruth dead and Laurence himself dying, there'd been no reason why he shouldn't have told him that he had a daughter in Australia. They could have discussed the situation together.

But Laurence had remained silent on the matter, choosing instead to drink wine and make idle conversation with Leonardo about *his* family's constant pressuring him to get married. Leonardo felt quite hurt that his friend hadn't confided in him about his secret daughter. Instead, he'd hurried off to London, changed his will then died without explaining why he'd structured his last wishes that way.

Leonardo could only speculate. He didn't *know*. He supposed it had to have been to get Veronica to come here personally. Though, there had been no guarantee of that. She could have sold the place from Australia and never darkened this doorstep. Still, Laurence wouldn't have thought of that. He really hadn't had a great imagination. If he'd decided something would happen a certain way, then it had to happen that way. It was as well that he'd made *him* executor of the will. Leonardo suspected that, if he hadn't met Veronica all those years ago, she might not have come to Capri.

What a terrible thought!

So was the thought that Veronica would soon be leaving. He wondered how he could persuade her to stay longer. It wasn't just the sex. It was her company—rather like having Laurence still here, only better.

He had just sat down at the computer again when Veronica returned.

'I didn't ring Mum,' she explained. 'I just sent her the photos and a text. She told me the other day that I didn't have to ring all the time and that I should just have a good holiday away from everything. I took her at her word this time. Did you find anything more on the computer?'

'No,' he replied, not wanting to admit that he hadn't even looked, that he'd been reading the report again.

'Oh, well. At least we have an idea now about why he left me his house. He must have known Mum would tell me he was my father and that I'd want to come here and find out all about him.'

Leonardo had his doubts about that, but declined to say so. Laurence had had a very unemotional way of looking at most things. His daughter had some of his pragmatism but, being a physiotherapist and not a geneticist, this possibly inherited characteristic had been softened by her more caring profession and her sex. She could be tough, he could see that. But she was still all woman, with a woman's tendency to surrender herself totally in bed. Just thinking about how she felt under him fired his testosterone once more. It pained him to think that one day she would just be a dim memory.

But she's not gone yet…

Leonardo walked over to her and took her in his arms. 'If he hadn't left you this villa,' he said, 'today would never have happened.'

'What a horrible thought,' she said, her voice teasing but her eyes sparking with instant desire.

'I'll get some pizzas delivered afterwards,' he pronounced as his mouth slowly descended.

'What about the wine cellar?'

His lips hovered above hers, his heart thundering in his chest as he fought for control. 'I'll take you down there afterwards as well. Though, you might find it a little chilly without your clothes on.'

He thrilled to her widening eyes, plus his recent knowledge that she wasn't nearly as sexually experienced as she'd pretended to be. Hell, he was the first man she'd slept with in three years. He vowed to make this weekend something she would never forget. But to do that he would have to concentrate on her pleasure, not his. Even now he could feel his body racing away with him.

He breathed in deeply, telling himself that making love was not the same as a downhill skiing competition. It was not a case of first to finish in the shortest possible time. It was more like ice-skating, where technique and artistry instead of speed won the day.

He kissed her slowly, doing his best to concentrate on *her* reactions and not his own. If only she hadn't wrapped her arms up around his neck. If only she hadn't pressed her breasts against him. If only she hadn't moaned…

It undid him, that moan.

To hell with taking things slowly! All thought of control was abandoned as he started stripping her where they stood.

CHAPTER TWENTY-TWO

'THIS IS ONE of the best pizzas I've ever tasted,' Veronica said truthfully as she took another large bite.

They were sitting out on the terrace, night having descended. They were fully dressed again, a necessity with the evening air having turned fresh.

'But of course,' Leonardo said smugly. 'It's Italian. But this wine is French.' And he picked up one of the glasses of red which sat on the small table between them.

He'd finally shown her where the cellar was, the entry behind a doorway that she'd mistaken for a closet. It was an enormous basement and, yes, chilly, with wall-to-wall shelves only half-filled with wine. Veronica had stared at the empty spots and felt sad at the thought of how much her father must have drunk to get liver cancer.

'I did know it was French,' she said with a roll of her eyes. 'Even an Aussie philistine like myself can recognise a French label when they see it. I'll have you know that I know a few Italian words as well.'

'Oh, really? Tell me some.'

'Let's see… There's *pizza*, and *arrivederci*, and *grazie*, and *bellissima*. And the best one of all. *Si*. I like that one. *Si*.'

'You'll be speaking like a native in no time,' he said drily.

'*Si,*' she repeated, her eyes smiling at him over the rim of her wine glass.

His eyes twinkled back at her.

'So how come you speak such good English?' she asked after she'd put her glass back down and picked up her slice of pizza.

'I did learn English at school. But I'd have to say my command of the language was mostly due to the fitness trainer my uncle hired for me when I became serious about my skiing. He was English and he refused to speak anything but English. His name was Hugh Drinkwater and he was quite a character. He was also a very bad skier. But that didn't matter. He wasn't teaching me to ski. I had a coach for that. He taught me the discipline of fitness. Believe me when I say there is no one better than an Englishman when it comes to discipline. He was ex-army and took no prisoners.'

'But you liked him,' she said, having heard the affection in his voice.

Her statement seemed to surprise him. 'Yes. Yes, I suppose I did. But he was a hard taskmaster.'

'A necessity with you, I would imagine, Leonardo.'

'What do you mean?'

'Come, now. You've been shockingly spoiled all your life. You would have needed someone tough to whip you into shape.'

He laughed. 'You could be right there.'

'I am right. So, what happened in the end? What were the injuries which forced you to retire before you wanted to?'

'Too many to enumerate. I broke practically every

bone you could break at one time or another. And pulled just about every muscle.'

'I read that you were a very reckless skier. But very brave,' she added, not wanting to offend him.

'I was a risk-taker, that's true. You have to take risks to win. Apparently, I took after my grandfather in that regard. Though his risks were in business, not on the ski slopes. My uncle inherited his talent for making money, but not my father. He hated the cut and thrust of the business world. When my grandfather died, *Papa* took his share of the money, put most of it into the bank and bought that hotel down there with the rest.' He nodded down the hillside to where the Hotel Fabrizzi stood. '*Papa's* a hard worker but he likes a simple life. Running a small hotel suits him.'

'And your mother?' Veronica asked. 'Does she like life on Capri?'

'She loves it. So do my sisters. I love it too, but only in small doses. It's too quiet for me. When they came to live here, I stayed in Milan with Uncle Stephano. I wanted to ski professionally and I couldn't do that from here. He sponsored me and taught me the textile business during the off season. There's nothing I don't know about manufacturing and selling fabrics.'

'Do you still miss it?' she asked. 'The skiing life?'

When he shrugged, she saw that that was what he did when he didn't want to answer a question, or face something.

'You couldn't do it for ever, Leonardo,' she pointed out. 'Age would have caught up with you, even if injuries didn't.'

'I would have liked to do it a little longer,' he bit out. 'I was favourite to become world champion that year.'

'We don't always get what we want in life, Leonardo,' she said with a touch of her old bitterness.

'True,' he said, not picking up on her change in mood. But it had changed, the happiness which Leonardo's company brought to her spoiled by thinking about Jerome's treachery.

She stood up abruptly, having found that doing things was the best antidote for unhappy thoughts. At home, she would distract herself with work. Housework, if she wasn't seeing a client at the time.

'What are you doing?' he asked her.

'Cleaning up,' she replied as she swept up the dirty plates.

'I can see that. But why? It can wait, can't it? You haven't finished your wine and I was enjoying our conversation.'

'Really?'

'Yes. Really. Talking to you is like talking to Laurence. He used to make me open up and tell him my worries. It's a relief sometimes to confide in someone else, especially someone nice and non-judgemental. And it's far cheaper than seeing a therapist.'

Veronica stood there, holding the plates, genuinely surprised by his admission.

'I can't imagine you ever seeing a therapist.'

'I did for a while. Being forced to retire affected me terribly. But, in the end, I realised that going over and over my feelings wasn't doing me any good, so I stopped.'

Veronica put the plates back down and settled back into her chair.

'Yes, I'm not sure that's the right way to get over things. The world seems obsessed with celebrating anniversaries at the moment, especially ones remember-

ing quite wretched events. I honestly think it's a bad
thing to dwell on the past. I did it for far too long. You
have to accept reality and then move on.'

Even as she said the brave words, Veronica recognised it was a case of easier said than done. After all,
until recently she'd hugged her misery around her like
a cloak, afraid to move on, afraid of some other man
hurting her as Jerome had done. But at least she had finally moved on. And she doubted Leonardo would hurt
her. She wouldn't let him, for starters, this last thought
crystallising her decision to end their fling tomorrow.
It was too much of a risk to keep on seeing him. He was
way too attractive. And way too good in bed.

But she wouldn't say anything until she had to. Hopefully, he wouldn't take it badly, or as a blow to his ego,
which was considerable.

Veronica picked up her wine glass and took a deep
swallow.

'You are meant to savour this type of red wine,'
Leonardo chided. 'Not drink it like water.'

'Ooh. Pardon me for breathing. I did tell you that I
prefer white wine but you insisted on my trying one of
the reds. Is this better?' she asked, lifting the glass to
her lips and taking a delicate sip.

'Much better. I apologise if I sound snobbish. It's just
that this particular wine is one of the best ever bottled
and needs to be sipped to be appreciated.'

'It *is* nicer when sipped. Okay, I forgive you.'

'*Grazie,*' he said, and smiled over at her.

Her heart lurched anew, warning bells going off in
her head.

Veronica searched her mind for the best subject to
quell any growing emotional involvement with this man.

'Tell me, Leonardo,' she said. 'On the night we first met, all those years ago, if I'd said yes would you have really enjoyed a threesome with me and that blonde bimbo?'

His dark eyes glittered. 'But of course. Though my mind would have been on you all the time. I wanted you like crazy.'

Veronica's fingers tightened around her wine glass. Why, oh, why had he had to add that last bit? 'Were you in the habit of having threesomes?' she asked stiffly.

'No. Like I told you, I was very drunk that night.'

'Your friends didn't seem shocked by your suggestion.'

'My friends were also pretty drunk. And stoned, some of them.'

'Yes, I noticed that.'

Leonardo sighed. 'It was a common thing in the circles I moved in.'

'And what about now? Do you take drugs now?'

'I never took drugs back then. I didn't like them.'

'I see…' Did she believe him? She supposed she had to, since he would have admitted it if he had taken them. He wouldn't see any reason to hide his actions.

'And what about you, Veronica? You went to university which, I am told, is rife with drugs. Did you ever indulge?'

'Never. I hate drugs.'

'That is a good thing. They ruin people's lives.'

'They certainly do,' she said.

They both fell silent for a few moments, Leonardo being the first to speak again.

'We are getting too serious. After we've finished our wine, we shall go back to bed.'

For a split second his presumption—and his arro-gance—annoyed her. But the thought of the pleasure that awaited her in bed with Leonardo trumped any sense of feminine outrage.

Whilst she sipped the rest of her wine, her mind was already there, naked in bed with him. The only con-cession she made to her pride was that, this time, *she* would be the one making love to him. First with her mouth, then with her whole body. *She* would be the one on top, with him at her mercy. She would thrill to his moans and wallow in his arousal. She would do to him what he'd done to her. She would not stop until he begged her to.

CHAPTER TWENTY-THREE

'I HAVE TO GO.'

Veronica looked up from where she was loading the dishwasher to see Leonardo standing there, showered and dressed with his overnight bag in his hand. She herself was still naked underneath her bathrobe.

'But you haven't even had breakfast yet,' she said on straightening.

Leonardo dropped the bag and come forward to take her into his arms. 'I know,' he murmured into her hair. 'But it's almost eleven. The hotel guests will have left and *Mamma* will be expecting me for Sunday lunch. After that, I have to return to Milan. I have an important meeting in the morning which I must attend. Still, it's best I go whilst you still have some reputation left. I will claim I slept in the guest room but I doubt anyone will believe me.'

She pulled back and lifted cool eyes to his. 'You told me I shouldn't care what other people think.'

'*Mamma* and *Papa* are not other people. They are my parents. Now, don't make a fuss. I will return. Though, not next weekend I'm afraid. I have things on.'

'What things?'

'A charity ball on the Saturday night which my company sponsors every year.'

'Oh. And I suppose you'll be going with some glamorous model on your arm?'

'No. I told you, I have no girlfriend in my life at the moment, other than you. If I asked you, would you come with me?'

Her heart fluttered at his invitation. She was seriously tempted, until she remembered her decision last night to end their affair today. It was a painful decision but a necessary one. 'I came here to find out about my father, Leonardo, not go flitting all over Italy to attend fancy dos. And I am not your girlfriend,' Veronica pointed out a little tartly.

'You could be. All you have to do is stay here in this villa and I will make Capri my second home.'

Exasperation joined temptation with this particular offer. Because it was a typically selfish suggestion on his part. He didn't want her on a for ever basis. He just hadn't had enough of what she'd given him last night. And, brother, she'd given him a lot!

'I don't think that would work, Leonardo,' she said archly. 'I'm not cut out to be mistress material.'

His dark eyes glittered. 'Oh, I wouldn't say that.'

'I would. Besides, what would your parents think? Not about me but about you. They would finally have to face up to the fact that you're an incorrigible playboy with no intention of getting married.'

'Maybe you could change my mind on that score.'

She laughed. 'Please don't insult my intelligence.'

His frown contained frustration. 'Why do you persist in thinking so badly of me?'

'Let's not argue, Leonardo. I've had a lovely time this weekend and I want to remember it fondly.'

'How long are you actually staying?'

'My return flight is in three weeks' time. I leave on a Sunday.'

'Then you'll still be here the weekend after next.'

'Yes...'

'What say you meet me in Rome that weekend? By then you will have found out everything you can about Laurence. I will show you the city and we'll have another great time together. My uncle has a lovely town-house he'll let us use. Or I can book us into a hotel.'

Don't say yes! came the savage warning from deep inside her. *You'll regret it.*

At least she didn't say yes straight away. There again, she didn't say no, either.

'I'll think about it,' was what she said.

He smiled, looking supremely confident in her saying yes in the end.

'I will ring you tonight.'

'Please don't.'

'I will ring you tonight,' he repeated, giving her a brief peck before picking up his bag and striding away, not glancing back over his shoulder even once.

She stared after him, her heart thudding fast in her chest, her head in a whirl. Because she was already looking forward to his call tonight.

Oh, Veronica. You should have told him no straight away. You should have put an end to this once and for all. Tell him tonight. Be strong. Be firm. Now, ring the airline and make an earlier booking. You need to go home ASAP. Before it's too late.

She didn't ring the airline, of course. She procrastinated, spending the next couple of hours going through the drawers in her father's desk, looking for Lord knew what. She didn't find anything enlightening, only the typical stuff you found in household drawers. Papers of every kind, copies of old bills, receipts for things bought over the years, pamphlets and brochures. There wasn't anything about her, or his will. After that, she tried to open his computer but it had shut down again, and she needed his password, which she didn't have. She hadn't thought to ask Leonardo to write it down but she would tonight, if and when he rang.

She wasn't so sure that he would ring. Out of sight was possibly out of mind where Leonardo was concerned. Not so in her own case. He was constantly in her mind, her thoughts troubling her. For they were no longer thoughts of lust but…dared she think it?… thoughts of love…?

Her memory recalled several times during the night when their love-making had taken on a highly emotional edge. At least for her it had, especially when she'd followed through with her idea to be the one in control. That was a laugh. She had never been in control. Not once, either of her body or her soul. It seemed it was impossible for her to be that intimate with this man and not have her heart join the proceedings.

Leonardo himself made it extremely difficult for her to remain the sexual sophisticate she'd vowed to be. His passion was her undoing, plus his tenderness, especially after she was recovering after yet another explosive climax. He would always hold her close and murmur sweet nothings in her ear. He didn't tell her he loved her, instead using other euphemisms which any foolish female would swoon to. Sometimes he talked to her in Italian, possibly saying dirty things. She had no way of knowing. But the words didn't sound dirty. They sounded…

romantic. No matter how much Veronica tried to tell herself this was just lust between them, she no longer believed it. Not on her side, anyway.

Leonardo, of course, was a different story. He was an accomplished seducer. And lover. A playboy, let her never forget. He operated in the bedroom on autopilot, knowing exactly what to say and do. Yes, he wanted to see her again. Why not when the chemistry between them was so good? Clearly, he hadn't had his fill yet.

Veronica knew that to spend another weekend with him, this time in Rome being wined, dined and romanced, would be very silly indeed. At the same time, how could she resist it?

Oh, Lord…

Sighing, Veronica rose from her father's desk and went in search of further distraction. She found some in a pile of photo albums she discovered on the top shelf of the linen press. They were numbered from one to five, tracing Laurence's life from when he'd been a baby. Veronica soon became engrossed in them, marvelling at how much they'd looked alike as infants before their different sexes had too much of an influence. It was also a shock to see a mirror image of herself in his mother. Clearly, the maternal genes had been the dominant ones, Laurence's father being a very ordinary-looking man with pale eyes and hair.

Each album showed her father at a different stage in his life. She went through them slowly, enjoying the glimpses into Laurence's life at various stages. His school years, then his days at university, where it seemed he must have been quite good at athletics. There were several photos of him running in races, a few of him crossing the line in first place. Veronica had been quite a good runner herself at school, though she preferred skiing.

Album number three was totally devoted to his wedding to Ruth and their honeymoon, which had obviously been spent in Italy. They'd toured most of the major cities, as well as visits to Sicily and Capri. Possibly this was where their love affair with the island had started. Album four covered the middle years of their marriage, with lots of pictures of Laurence at work and Ruth in her garden. Veronica gasped when she saw a group shot taken at a party, with her mother in the background serving drinks. What surprised her most was that she was smiling. It made Veronica wonder if this was after she'd fallen pregnant. Nora had always claimed that the day she'd found out she was expecting was the happiest day of her life. Laurence wasn't in the same photograph, but Ruth was, smiling her usual warm smile at the camera.

Album five followed the later years of their marriage, including snaps of various holidays, plus lots of the renovations they'd made to this villa. It had been a bit of a wreck when they'd bought it, though the view had always been great. This last album wasn't full, ending abruptly with a photo of Ruth looking very fragile, and Laurence hovering protectively behind her chair, his violet eyes worried.

Veronica suspected that Laurence's will to live had died with his wife's death. She wouldn't mind betting that that was when he'd started drinking heavily. Sad, really. If only he'd reached out to *her* instead of killing himself slowly. They could have become friends. She could have given him a reason to live. Instead, he'd just withered on the vine, so to speak, not caring about his health or his long-lost daughter. Leonardo seemed to be the only person in the world he cared about. And that was possibly only surface caring.

Or was it?

Veronica's anger at her father's actions regarding herself was making her judge him harshly with others. Clearly, he'd been very fond of Leonardo. And very trusting of him as a man. You didn't make a person executor of your will if you didn't have good faith in their integrity and honesty.

Honesty and integrity were not words she normally associated with playboys. Yet, strangely, they did seem to apply to Leonardo. Just because he wasn't in a hurry to marry and have children didn't mean he wasn't a good person. He had remarked more than once that she had no reason to think so badly of him. Veronica vowed to be fairer in her assessment of his character in future. Though fairer did not mean stupider. It was still risky to keep on seeing him. She really didn't want to fall for him any more deeply than she already had. At the moment, her heart was still relatively safe. Leaving Leonardo would hurt, but she would survive.

As Veronica closed the last album and put it on top of the pile, something slipped out of the back pages and fluttered to the ground. It was a small photograph, she saw on picking it up. Of herself as a newborn baby. On the back was written her name, her date of birth and her birth weight. Nothing else.

Had her mother sent it? Or had her father hired another detective agency all those years ago?

Only one way to find out for sure, she supposed.

Veronica carried the photograph into the bedroom where she'd left her phone. She tried to work out what time it was in Australia but she had no idea; her brain seemed to have gone on holiday. She'd just have to take a chance that her mother wasn't asleep, because she simply couldn't wait.

Her mother answered fairly quickly, and without sounding fuzzy.

'You're still awake,' Veronica said, guessing that it had to be close to midnight.

'I never go to bed too early. You know that. What's wrong?'

'Nothing's wrong. I just need to ask you something.'

'What?'

'Did you send my father a photograph of me after I was born?'

'What? Oh, yes, actually, I did. It was one of his conditions. But I wasn't to send it to his house. It went to his place of work back in London. He was worried that his wife might find it by mistake.'

'So he did care about me, then?'

A heavy sigh wafted down the line. 'I suppose so, love.'

'Why do you doubt it?'

'It was just something he said at the time, back when he found out I was pregnant. He seemed keen to see how much you were like him. He had this thing for passing on good genes, as you know. He lived and breathed his work.'

Veronica pulled a face. 'Sounds like I was just an experiment for him.'

'No, no, I wouldn't go that far. It was only natural that Laurence would be interested in seeing what you looked like. You have to understand…he probably would have liked to have a relationship with you.

To love you like a real father. But he couldn't. He was hamstrung by his love for his wife. He adored her. She came first with him.'

'Then why didn't he contact me after she died?' Veronica snapped.

'I don't know, love. Oh, please don't get all worked up about this. Life and relationships are complex things. And people don't always do the right thing. I dare say Laurence regretted a lot of things in the end. Maybe he tried to make up for his absence in your life by leaving you that villa,' her mother suggested. 'You have to admit, it's a very beautiful place.'

Veronica opened her mouth to tell her mother he'd had her investigated recently, but then decided against it. She needed to think about her father's reasons for doing what he had without her mother confusing her with endless speculations.

'Maybe he didn't expect you to sell it,' Nora went on regardless. 'Maybe he wanted you to live there.'

'Maybe. I guess we'll never know now, Mum,' Veronica said, hoping to stop her mother from any further speculating. 'Anyway, I can't live here. Not permanently.' She could not bear the thought of running into Leonardo whenever he came home, or being within a short plane trip of wherever he was.

'Why not rent it out as a holiday place? You'd get a good rental. And then you could holiday there yourself occasionally.'

'No, Mum. I need to come home,' she said firmly.

Her mother was always good at picking up her feelings. 'It's because of that man, isn't it?' she said sharply. 'Leonardo Fabrizzi.'

'Yes, Mum.'

'You haven't fallen for him, have you?'

'I think I might have. A little.' She gave a dry laugh. 'Actually, more than a little. So I need to get out of here before it gets more serious. On my side, that is. Leonardo isn't the kind of man to get serious over any woman.'

'Oh, dear. It's all my fault, telling you to get out there and have fun. I should have known you'd be extra vulnerable after all these years of having no man in your life.'

'It's not your fault, Mum. I'm just a fool. Anyway, I'm going to ring the airlines and move my flight forward a week. So expect me home on Friday week. There's no risk before then. Leonardo can't make it back here until that weekend, by which time I'll be safely gone.'

'Lord. You make it sound like you're afraid of him.'

'Not of him, Mum. Of my own silly self.'

'Is he that irresistible?'

Veronica closed her eyes, her mind immediately conjuring up an image of him looming over her in bed last night, his dark eyes glittering wildly, his voice rough with desire as he told her what he was going to do to her. All night long.

'He is to me,' Veronica choked out. And possibly to all the swathes of women who'd come before her.

'Then you had better come home.'

CHAPTER TWENTY-FOUR

BY THE TIME Leonardo picked up his car at Milan airport he'd come to the conclusion that he was actually falling in love for the first time in his life. He'd missed Veronica like mad within minutes of leaving her. At first, he'd put his feelings down to missing the fantastic sex they'd had together, not realising that his feelings came from something way deeper than that.

Lunch with his parents had been tedious as he tried to sidestep their escalating hopes over his relationship with Veronica. He'd lied, saying that they weren't romantically involved, but he could see they weren't buying it. They kept looking at each other with that knowing glint in their eyes until in the end he stopped bothering with the lies, saying instead that, yes, he liked Veronica a lot, but she was going home to Australia in three weeks' time and there was no point in pursuing the girl. He scoffed at the suggestion that he invite her to stay with him in Milan for a while.

He was no longer scoffing at that idea. In fact, he thought it was a very good idea. He could not wait to ring her and suggest it. It was a pity that the ski season hadn't started yet. Then he could have taken her skiing. But no matter. There were many other places he could take her. Venice, perhaps. Girls loved the romance of Venice.

By the time Leonardo arrived home—he owned a house not that far from the airport—he could hardly contain his excitement. Of course, he couldn't tell her he loved her. Yet. That would be premature. And not conducive to achieving his goal, which was her loving him back. He could see Veronica was wary of relationships, though why that was, he wasn't sure. Her fiancé had been killed. He hadn't run off with some other woman. The hurt he sometimes glimpsed in her eyes when talking about men must have come from some other earlier man's treatment of her.

Yes. That had to be it.

Leonardo hurried inside, the house very quiet. He always gave his housekeeper the weekend off when he went to Capri. Francesca was a widow in her fifties and lived in most of the time, but on her weekends off she liked to visit her daughter who lived in Florence, so she wouldn't be back until the morning. A glance at his Rolex showed it wasn't too late to call Veronica. It was only twenty-past nine. Pulling out his phone, he hurried upstairs and lay down on his bed, stretching out before bringing up her number and hitting the dial icon.

She took her time answering. The thought that she'd seen who was ringing and simply didn't want to answer was a worrying one.

'Hi,' she said at last. 'I'm glad you rang.'

His spirits rose immediately.

'I have something I wanted to ask you,' she went on, her voice brisk and businesslike, reminding him of the voice she'd used when she'd discussed arrangements with him over the phone from Australia. It made him rethink his tactics, knowing instinctively that she wasn't just going to say yes to what he wanted. Maybe he should concentrate on getting her to come to Rome in a fortnight's time. Asking her to come visit him in Milan seemed a step too far at this early stage.

'What is it?' he replied, trying not to sound crestfallen, which was something Leonardo rarely felt when it came to women.

'I need the password to Laurence's computer,' she said.

Leonardo frowned. 'What for?'

'I've been going through his things. I thought I should go through his computer as well, have a look at his search history. It might give me a few clues.'

'Clues to what?'

'To why he left me this place, for starters,' she said sharply. 'Which reminds me, what happened to his phone?'

'His phone?'

'Yes. I would imagine my father was well up on technology. He was an intelligent man. He would have carried a smart phone with him everywhere.'

'Yes, he did. I have it in a drawer at work, along with his wallet and his watch.'

'Oh.'

'If you want them, I could give them to you when we meet up in Rome,' he offered.

Her hesitation to answer straight away was telling. Leonardo's heart sank.

'I… I haven't made up my mind about that yet,' she said carefully.

At least she hadn't said no outright. Still, Leonardo

wasn't used to women waffling where his invitations were concerned. He wasn't sure what to say next.

'If you don't fancy Rome, then how about Venice?'

'Venice?' she echoed.

'Yes. The city of love.'

'I thought that was Paris,' she returned, her voice quite cool, making him instantly regret his use of the word.

'You sound like you're not too keen,' he said, knowing that *he* sounded put out, but unable to harness his disappointment.

'I told you, Leonardo. I think it's best we don't keep seeing each other.'

'You don't really mean that.'

'You're just not used to girls turning you down.'

'Possibly. But I honestly believe we have something special. I'd like to explore things further between us.'

She laughed. She actually laughed. 'I know the kind of exploring you mean and I'm sorry, Leonardo—I do find you terribly attractive, but I can't see any future for us.'

'How do you know?'

'I just know.'

'Is it my playboy reputation which worries you?'

'Partly.'

'I'm not as bad as the media make out.'

'If you say so.'

She didn't sound convinced and Leonardo was beginning to despair. So he played his trump card.

'What if you're the right girl Laurence said would come along one day?'

He heard her suck in her breath sharply.

'You're just saying that,' she bit out.

'No,' he said firmly. 'I'm not. Look, I'm as surprised as you are. But surely you can see the chemistry between us is stronger than usual?'

She said nothing, though he could hear her breathing down the line. It was very fast.

'For pity's sake, you can't go back to Australia without giving us the chance to find out our true feelings for each other.'

'You promise me you're not just saying this to get me into bed again?'

'Cross my heart and hope to die.'

Her sigh was long. 'If you're playing with me, Leonardo, then you just might die. By my hands.'

Her passionate words excited him. And gave him confidence. She must care about him to feel that strongly.

'I'm not playing with you,' he reassured her.

'I hope not.'

'I can see you have had your trust in men severely damaged. I can only think some man in your past treated you very badly. A player, is my guess. Am I right?'

'Yes and no. He wasn't what you would call a player, just an extremely selfish man who thought of no one's wishes but his own.'

'And you think I'm like that, thinking of no one's wishes but my own?'

'*Don't* you?'

'No,' he denied hotly. Though he suspected he was guilty of some selfishness.

'In that case, please do not ring me again until next Sunday evening, at which point I will give you my answer about the following weekend.'

'What harm could there possibly be in my ringing

you? I like talking to you, Veronica. You don't sugar-coat your answers. You certainly don't flatter me the way most women usually do.'

'*You're* using flattery now to get your own way.'

He ground his teeth with frustration. 'You constantly misread me.'

'I don't think so, Leonardo, but you could prove your good intentions by doing what I ask.'

'Very well,' he bit out. 'I won't ring you until next Sunday evening.' With that he hung up, too annoyed with her even to say goodbye. Lord, but she was one difficult woman!

CHAPTER TWENTY-FIVE

VERONICA DIDN'T SLEEP well that night, tossing and turning until well after midnight, then waking with the dawn. For a long time she lay there, thinking about Leonardo. Already she was regretting her tough stance of the night before, knowing full well that when next Sunday came she would say yes to spending the following weekend with him. Which meant she wouldn't be ringing the airlines today and changing her flight to an earlier one.

The romantic side of her wanted to believe he was falling in love with her, but the sensible, pragmatic side kept warning her that it was too good to be true. It was just as well, she decided in the end, that she'd forbidden him to ring her this week. At least that way she wouldn't be swayed by his sexy voice and, yes, his flattery. Veronica vowed to keep her head and to use this week to do what she'd come here to do: find out everything she could about her father.

It was a stroke of luck that at eleven that morning, after Veronica had spent hours going through her father's computer without finding a single enlightening thing—he obviously only used it for the most basic correspondence and banking—the front doorbell was rung by the one person who possibly knew more about Laurence than anyone else living on Capri.

Carmelina, Leonardo's sister and Laurence's part-time housekeeper.

'Good morning, Veronica,' she said when Veronica opened the sliding glass door, her English more formal than her brother's. 'I am sorry if I woke you.'

Veronica sashed her bathrobe and smiled at Carmelina. 'You haven't. I've been up for hours. I was just too lazy to get dressed.'

Carmelina smiled back. She was in her mid- to late thirties and still very attractive—as all the Fabrizzis were—with dark eyes and hair and the loveliest olive skin.

Good genes, her father would have said. Veronica smiled at the thought, pleased that she could think of her father without feeling frustrated with him.

'I have come to do the cleaning,' Carmelina said. 'Leonardo. He is a messy boy. He drops towels and does not pick up.'

'Oh, no, no, no,' Veronica said. 'I couldn't possibly let you do that. I am quite capable of doing my own cleaning. Trust me. I am not *that* lazy. I have all day and nothing much else to do. But, now that you're here, I would like to talk to you. About my father,' she added quickly when Carmelina looked a little alarmed.

They had coffee together out on the terrace, Carmelina also admiring the view, despite no doubt having seen it countless times. The day was warmer than the previous day, and the sea breeze delightfully cooling.

'I wish I didn't have to sell this place,' Veronica said.

'Do you have to? I would like you to live here. You would be a very nice neighbour.'

'I can't afford the taxes,' she said, having realised that proving Laurence was her father would be virtually impossible. There wasn't a single personal item of his in his bedroom or bathroom, everything having been cleared out and the whole house thoroughly cleaned.

'If you married Leonardo,' Carmelina said, 'he would pay the taxes. He is very rich.'

Veronica smiled at the wonderful simplicity of Carmelina's solution. If only life was that straightforward. 'You all want Leonardo to get married, don't you?'

'*Si,*' Carmelina said. 'But only to someone nice. Like you.'

'We've only just met, Carmelina.'

'No matter. I love my Alfonso the first day I meet him. Leonardo likes you very much. I can tell.'

'Yes, but…'

'You like him too.'

'I do, but…'

Carmelina frowned over at her, waiting for her to continue.

'I don't think Leonardo is ready for marriage yet.'

'Oh, pah! He is ready. He just needs a push.'

'Pushing doesn't always work, Carmelina. Not with someone like Leonardo. He has to make up his own mind. You should tell your mother and father to back off.'

'Laurence thought he needed a push.'

'What? What did you say?'

'I said Laurence thought my brother was ready for a wife. He said he just needed the right girl. Maybe he was thinking of you, Veronica.'

It was a stunning thought, and one which Veronica would never have imagined. But it was possible, she supposed. Maybe that was why he'd left her this villa. And why he'd made Leonardo the executor of his will. So that they could meet and fall in love. It was a hopelessly romantic idea which seemed uncharacteristic of what she'd learned about Laurence.

But maybe it was true. It certainly appealed to her own romantic side.

'Tell me, Carmelina, what kind of man was my father?'

Carmelina tipped her head on one side as she considered her answer.

'He was very English,' she said at last. 'He did not like to show his feelings. Not like Italians. When his wife died, he did not cry. He just sat out here and did not speak. For days and days.'

Veronica's heart turned over. 'Oh, how sad.'

'Yes, that was what he was. Sad. Very sad.'

'Was that when he started to drink too much?'

'*Si*. He try to hide it but I see the empty bottles.'

Tears pricked at Veronica eyes. *If only he'd contacted me*, she thought. *If only he...*

She stood up abruptly. 'I don't think I want to talk about that any more.'

Carmelina shook her head as she stood up also. 'You are just like him. You are afraid to show your feelings. Come. You need a hug.'

The rest of the day went very well. Carmelina helped Veronica give the house a quick tidy-up while the sheets and towels were in the washing machine. After remaking the bed with fresh linen and replacing the damp towels with fresh ones, Veronica jumped in the shower. Half an hour later both girls left the house arm in arm to go shopping.

Not for clothes or even food. It was more of a look-but-not-buy expedition where Carmelina showed Veronica the best places to buy both, as well as the easiest ways for her to get around. They walked some, caught a bus and finally, when they were tired, they called Franco to come, pick them up and drive them home.

'You ladies look like you have fun,' he said in his usual jolly manner.

'We did, Franco,' Veronica assured him. 'Carmelina was a marvellous guide. Almost as good as you,' she added with a sparkling smile.

Franco beamed, catching her eye in the rear-view mirror. '*Si.* I am the most best guide on Capri. With the best car too. You call me any time you need ride, Veronica. I will not charge you.'

'Ooh. I will tell Elena,' Carmelina said cheekily.

'She will not care. Elena knows I love her. She not jealous.'

Carmelina laughed. 'She's very jealous of any pretty girl who smiles at you.'

Veronica grinned. 'Then I will try not to smile at him when he gives me a lift.'

'*Si.* Good idea.'

Franco drove round to the delivery entrance to the villa, probably to avoid his wife seeing Veronica in his car. But Veronica was just grateful that she didn't have to climb those steep steps. Her new sandals were starting to rub and she suspected she might have the beginnings of blisters. Saying goodbye to both Franco and Carmelina, she took herself wearily inside, ready to have a siesta. It wasn't late—only three—but Carmelina had wanted to get back before the children arrived home from school.

Veronica immediately went down to the bedroom where she dropped her bag by the bed, slipped off her sandals and crashed onto the cover, sleep finding her in less than a minute. When she woke the light outside showed that the sun was very low in the sky. Sighing, she rolled over and reached for her bag, rifling through it for her phone. Once retrieved she checked the time. Six twenty-three. She'd been asleep for over three hours.

She rose and made her way to the bathroom. It wasn't until then that the thought occurred to Veronica that her period hadn't arrived yet. She wasn't overly worried. Although her period was usually as regular as clockwork, her poor body had been through the mill lately, what with the shock of finding out about Laurence, followed by the nervous exhaustion of travelling here, not knowing what she would discover.

Veronica suddenly recalled how her reproductive system had shut down for a while after Jerome had died. This might be something similar. It didn't cross her mind that she might have fallen pregnant. The thought did occur to her, however, that if her cycle had been disturbed she would have to ask Leonardo to use condoms, if and when she went away with him again. Which could present a problem. What reason could she give when she'd already had unprotected sex with him many times?

Oh, dear. Perhaps she just shouldn't go away with him. After all, her female intuition kept warning her that he was all hot air about their sexual chemistry being extra special, implying that he might be falling in love with her.

Unfortunately, at the same time, her own feelings kept overriding common sense, tapping into his appeal to give him a chance to show her he wasn't the player she thought he was. It would be difficult to deny him that chance when she was absolutely crazy about him.

But if he put a foot wrong that weekend then that would be that. And putting a foot wrong could include making a fuss when she asked him to use protection. If he cared for her as he said he did, then he should just do as she wanted, no questions asked.

Suddenly she regretted demanding he not ring her until Sunday. She would so like to hear his voice. Dared she ring him herself?

No. Perhaps not. Nothing good ever came of a girl seeming too eager. She would content herself with reading one of the very interesting looking novels her father had in his bookshelf next to his desk. It seemed he'd liked spy stories, a genre which had never overly appealed to her. But she supposed if her father had liked them then maybe so would she. So she selected a medium-sized tome with the provocative title of *One Spy Too Many* and took it out onto the terrace. There she settled, soon engrossed in what turned out to be a real page-turner.

It was hunger pains which finally forced Veronica to lift her eyes from the book. That, and the light fading so much that she was forced to go inside if she wanted to continue to read whilst she ate. Either that or turn on the outside lights. But that always attracted insects.

Dinner was poached eggs on toast. More of a breakfast than a dinner meal but it was enough for now. She'd had a huge plate of pasta at lunchtime. She hadn't come to Italy to get fat, though it would be easy...the food was so delicious.

When her period still hadn't arrived by the time she'd

finished the book late that night, Veronica resigned herself to her cycle temporarily having gone walkabout. When it had happened before she'd gone to the doctor in a panic, thinking she'd contracted some dreaded disease, but after an examination and some tests the doctor had told her that she was perfectly fine. The worst thing she could do, the doctor had said, was worry. His advice had been to eat healthily, take plenty of exercise and do things she enjoyed. Which had been a little hard back then when nothing had made her happy.

Not so on the Isle of Capri.

Veronica decided to follow that doctor's instructions to a T. The next morning she rose early and went for a walk before breakfast. Nothing too adventurous, just down the road and back again. Then after breakfast she made her way carefully down the steep path to the Hotel Fabrizzi and asked Elena—who was sitting at a computer behind the reception desk in the coolly spacious foyer—if there was a map of Capri she could borrow. Elena showed her a stand on the wall which contained maps, as well as lots of brochures of tourist activities on Capri. Veronica sorted through them and took one of everything which interested her.

'Thank you, Elena,' she said.

'You are welcome,' came her warm reply. '*Mamma* said if I saw you to ask you to come to dinner tonight. Nothing like the other night. It will just be her and *Papa*.'

'How nice of her. That would lovely. Is she here?'

'She is busy doing the rooms with Carmelina at the moment. Can I say you will come?'

'Of course. What time do you think?'

'Seven. And don't eat too much before you come. *Mamma* likes to feed her guests until they burst.'

Veronica laughed. 'Yes. I did notice that last Friday night.'

'Have you heard from Leonardo?' Elena suddenly asked.

'He rang me on Sunday night to thank me for letting him stay. But not since then.'

Elena frowned. 'He was strange at lunch on Sunday.'

'Strange? What do you mean?'

'I do not know. He was not the brother I am used to. He was too quiet. I wondered if you had argued with him.'

'No. Not at all.'

'*Mamma* does not understand Leonardo. She and *Papa* keep pressing him to marry but he is not ready to settle down yet.'

'Leonardo will never be ready to settle down,' Veronica said, any foolish dreams she'd been harbouring totally shattered by voicing the truth out loud.

Elena's eyes showed her surprise. 'You know him well enough already to know that?'

'We met briefly many years ago,' Veronica explained. 'I knew then what kind of man he was.'

'He is a not a bad man,' Elena defended hotly, dark eyes flashing.

'No, but he is restless. And dissatisfied with his life. He never got over his retirement from competitive skiing. I hope your *mamma* and *papa* don't think he's going to marry *me*. Because he won't.'

Elena sighed. 'They must have hope, Veronica. Please don't say any of this to them tonight.'

'Okay. I'll just play happy tourist.'

'You are more than a tourist. You are Laurence's daughter.'

Veronica left the hotel with her map and several brochures, troubled by her conversation with Elena. Perhaps because she'd finally accepted that loving a man like Leonardo was a sure path to misery.

Seeking distraction, she set herself the task of familiarising herself with all the established walks, as well as exploring the towns of Capri and Anacapri. Both were beautiful towns—quaint and historical—but she preferred Anacapri because it was smaller and out of reach of the day-trippers. She sat down at an *al fresco* table in the piazza there and had a lovely lunch—though not too big, given she was going to the Fabrizzis' for dinner that night. After lunch she bought a bottle of water and set off for another walk which took her down a steep, winding path to the most delightful little beach. There she sat on a smooth rock for a couple of hours, sandals off, her hot feet cooling in the tepid water.

The walk back up was not so delightful, but she took her time, though vowing not to do quite so much the following day. Her period still hadn't come but she'd decided not to worry about it. She couldn't *will* it to come, could she?

Once back at the villa, she had a long shower, followed by a short nap before dressing for dinner. Nothing too fancy, just a pair of black cotton culottes and a black-and-white wrap-around top that had elbow-length bat-wing sleeves. She left her hair down, having freshly washed and styled it.

'How lovely you look,' Sophia gushed before giving her the obligatory hug. 'But you have caught the sun, have you not?'

'I have,' Veronica confessed. 'I was silly and took off my hat while I was at a beach. The breeze and the water tricked me into thinking I was cool.'

'A little sun doesn't do any harm,' Alberto said, and came forward to give her a hug also.

Veronica wondered if she'd ever get used to all the hugging, then realised she wouldn't have to. Soon, she'd be back home in Australia and back to her less demonstrative lifestyle.

It was a rather depressing thought.

'We do not have any guests in the hotel tonight,' Sophia told her. 'We can eat in the dining room, if you wish. Or on the big table in the kitchen.'

'Oh, please, in the kitchen.'

Sophia beamed at her, her wide smile very satisfied. 'Good. Come. Alberto wishes to give you some of Alfonso's prized limoncello before we eat.'

'It is very good,' Alberto said. 'You will like.'

She did like. And she said so.

'Alfonso also makes his own wine,' Alberto added.

'He's very clever, then,' Veronica said.

The table in the kitchen was quite large. Sophia had set just one end with Alberto at the head and herself and Sophia flanking him. The food,, as Veronica had expected, was simply delicious, but not too over the top, just a meatball and spaghetti dish, all washed down with what she suspected was some of Alfonso's home-made wine. Dessert was a coconut cake which was very tasty. The coffee afterwards was strong, but Veronica didn't say anything, just added cream and sugar and gave up the idea of sleeping until the wee hours of the morning.

Not that it mattered. She didn't have to go anywhere tomorrow.

The meal ended around nine, Veronica surprised that not once had Sophia and Alberto brought up the subject of their son. In turn, she resisted the temptation to question them about her father, deciding she wanted just to enjoy their company and forget about everything else for tonight. They asked her about her job, which she explained, confessing that she worked six, sometimes seven days a week. They looked horrified, claimed she must be in need of a holiday, then made a lot of suggestions about how she should spend the rest of her time on Capri. They insisted she see the Blue Grotto again, but warned her to go very early in the day or very late, so that she didn't get caught up with all the day-trippers. Also on the list was the chairlift up the mountain, both of which she agreed to do.

After another round of hugs, and a promise to join the whole family for lunch next Sunday, Veronica left to walk home slowly, thinking what lovely parents Leonardo had. Much nicer than Jerome's parents.

Jerome…

For the first time in three years, Veronica was able to think about Jerome without feeling one bit upset, or even bitter. Finally, she was able to look at what he had done more objectively. Yes, it had been wicked of him to lie to her about loving her when he had loved another woman—a married doctor with whom he had worked. Even more wicked to plan to marry her and have children with her because he wanted a family, because the so-called love of his life refused to leave her husband and children and marry him. At the same time, she hadn't wanted to give Jerome up. She'd wanted to have her cake and eat it too. Veronica would never have found out the horrible truth if the woman hadn't broken down at Jerome's wake and confessed everything.

Veronica still hated Jerome and his lover, but they no longer had the power to destroy *her* life. She was free of them at last.

She had her father to thank for that. Her father and, yes, Leonardo.

A sigh came to her lips, a sigh for a dream which she accepted was just a dream. Leonardo wasn't going to change. Leopards didn't change their spots. He was taken with her because she was different, that was all. And maybe she was taken with him because he was different from the Australian boyfriends she'd had. Not just better looking but more passionate. More…exotic. And definitely more erotic.

A shiver ran down her spine when she thought of how much she loved the ways he made love to her. Nothing seemed wrong to her when she was in his arms.

Another sigh wafted from her lips, this one the sound of resignation.

There was no use pretending she could resist the temptation to spend another weekend with him, especially if she could spend it with him in Venice. She would insist on that. If she was going to risk another broken heart, then she could at least have it broken in Venice.

Her mind made up, she decided to tell him the good news when he rang her on Sunday evening.

CHAPTER TWENTY-SIX

By the time Friday morning came, Veronica really started to worry about her missing period. It was no use. She couldn't help it. She knew the odds of her being pregnant were very small, but not impossible. Her stomach somersaulted at the thought.

Because what if she *was* pregnant? Lord, what a disaster!

Logic told her she was panicking for nothing, but logic didn't always figure in life. She kept telling herself that she didn't *feel* pregnant. There was no lightheadedness, or being sick in the mornings, or swollen nipples. Of course, all those symptoms usually came later, not after just one week.

Sighing, she arose and dressed, still not having fulfilled her bucket list of activities for Capri. This morning she planned to go on the chairlift up the mountain, then later in the afternoon she would take a trip out to the Blue Grotto. Sandwiched in between she would walk, walk and walk some more. If nothing else, all the walking should make her sleep tonight. She didn't want to lie there worrying about having Leonardo's baby growing inside her body.

It would have been a marvellous day, Veronica

thought as she finally trudged up the steps to the villa just after six, if that last horrific thought hadn't plagued her mind every five minutes. Not that having a baby was horrific. It was having *Leonardo's* baby that horrified her. Because the stupid man would offer to marry her. And the last man on earth she wanted to be married to was a playboy—hardly a recipe for happiness for ever. Okay, so she was in love with the man. Stupidly. Hopelessly. And, yes, if there was to be a child, she would be severely tempted to say yes if he proposed. After all, she had personal experience of growing up without a father and she wouldn't wish that on any child.

And in truth Leonardo would probably be a good father. But he would be a hopeless husband. And undoubtedly unfaithful. That was something she could not bear, not after her experience with Jerome. If and when she married, she wanted her husband to be so besotted with her that he would not even *look* at another woman.

Veronica retrieved the key from the geranium pot, let herself in, dumped her hat and bag on the lounge then walked over to the kitchen area. There, she put on some water for coffee before heading for the bathroom, where a visit to the toilet showed nothing of note.

Naturally.

Cursing under her breath, she flushed the toilet, washed her hands and went back to make herself the coffee. Cradling the mug in her hands, she wandered out to the terrace in the hope of finding some peace with the soothing water view. She didn't. For the first time since coming here, she found no pleasure whatsoever in gazing out at the Mediterranean. Her mind was too full of worry to find pleasure in anything. She was severely tempted to ring her mother and talk things out with her.

They were very close, and rarely kept their problems from each other. Not only that, her mother was much less emotional than she was, and not given to dramatising situations or making mountains out of molehills.

The intelligent part of Veronica's brain told her that the odds of her being pregnant were very low. But she needed someone else to reassure her that she was panicking unnecessarily. So, as she sat there sipping her coffee, she worked out what time it was in Australia. All you had to do, she'd discovered after putting the question into her father's computer, was take off two hours from the current time, then change the a.m. to p.m. and vice versa. By eight tonight, it would be six in the morning in Australia, the time her mother usually rose come rain, hail or shine.

It was just after seven here now, and Veronica decided to get herself something to eat. By the time she picked up the phone an hour later, a nervous tension was gripping her stomach. She didn't want to worry her mother with what was possibly a non-existent problem but she desperately needed her advice.

'Veronica?' her mother answered. 'I didn't expect to hear from you. What's up?'

Trust her mother to twig straight away that there was something wrong.

'Nothing, I hope.'

'That sounds ominous.'

'Sorry, I'm not trying to alarm you. I just want to run something by you. Mum, you know how I'm always very regular. With my period, I mean.'

'Yes…' her mother said warily.

Veronica sighed. 'Well, I'm late.'

'Ah.'

'Yes, ah. I don't think I'm pregnant, but it is possible if ovulation was delayed.'

'Are you telling me you had unprotected sex with a playboy?'

She sounded aghast. And highly disapproving.

Veronica steeled herself. 'Yes. I'm afraid so.'

'Oh, for pity's sake! How come? I would have thought this Leonardo Fabrizzi would be more careful than that.'

'The first time, it just sort of happened. I mean…we both got carried away.'

'That doesn't sound like you.'

'It's not. But I did. Then when Leonardo came to his senses he asked me if an unwanted pregnancy was on the cards. I told him it wasn't. At the time I assumed I'd already ovulated. The trouble was *he* assumed I was on the pill.'

'And you let him think it.'

'Yes.'

'After which he was happy not to use a condom, like any man.'

'Yes,' she said again, but this time with a deep sigh. 'Oh, dear…'

'You think I'm pregnant, don't you?'

'Not necessarily. But it's well known that a girl is always extra vulnerable to a man at the time she ovulates. It's Mother Nature.'

Veronica began to feel sick.

'Look, that might not be the reason you lost your head over this man. You did say he was pretty irresistible.'

'He is.'

'You'd have to be very unlucky to be pregnant. Look, why don't you buy a pregnancy testing kit and find out one way or another?'

'I can't do that. Not here on Capri. Everyone knows everyone on this island. It would soon get around and Leonardo's parents might hear.' She shuddered at the thought. 'Anyway, it's way too early to get a reliable result.'

'Not necessarily. I saw a show on TV that said those tests can tell pretty early these days.'

'I suppose I could catch a ferry over to the mainland and buy one there.'

'Buy two. That way, you can take a test a few days apart and be sure.'

'That's a good idea. Thanks a lot, Mum. You always know what to do.'

'Not always. But at least it would put your mind at rest. Now, are you still coming home early, or has that idea gone by the board?'

'I'm not sure now. I haven't changed the flight yet.'

'Let me know what you decide. And what the results of the test are. What do you think you'll do if you are pregnant?'

'Come straight home.'

'And do what?'

'I don't know yet. I'll cross that bridge when I come to it.'

CHAPTER TWENTY-SEVEN

Negative. *It was* negative!

Veronica stared at the testing stick for a long time before dropping it on the bathroom floor then burying her face in her hands. *Oh, thank God, thank God.*

After a few sobs of relief, Veronica dropped her hands from her face, picked up the stick and threw it into the small bin under the vanity.

It wasn't that she didn't want a baby. Just not Leonardo's. At least, not right now. If by some miracle he was genuinely in love with her and wanted a future with her then, yes, having his baby would be the best thing in the world. She'd always wanted children, but only after she was married. No way did she want to go down the single mother road, like her own mother.

Not that she could be absolutely sure yet that she wasn't pregnant, she thought as she stripped off and stepped into the shower. It was still early days. But the girl in the chemist yesterday—it was called a *farmacia* in Italy—had assured Veronica that this particular test was the latest and best and could detect a pregnancy as early as a week. Given it was now Sunday morning, nine days after she and Leonardo had first had sex, then the test should be accurate. But she would take the test again in a few days, having followed her mother's advice to buy two kits.

But she wouldn't worry about that today. Today, she could at least go to lunch with the Fabrizzi family without having to pretend that everything was fine. But first she would text her mother with the good news.

'Veronica,' Elena whispered to her during dessert. They were sitting next to each other in the middle of the long table under the pergola, with children on either side.

'What?' Veronica whispered back, immediately tensing up at the urgency in Elena's voice.

'I need to speak to you after lunch. Alone.'

'All right.'

About what? Veronica wondered, her stomach rolling over with sudden alarm. *Nothing good, that's for sure.*

Finally, after lunch was over and all the thank-yous and goodbye hugs had taken place, Veronica looked at Elena and said, 'Would you have the time to walk back with me, Elena? I know you must be good with technology since you do all the bookings for the hotel and I need some help with Laurence's computer.'

Elena smiled at her inventiveness. 'Yes, of course. Franco, would you look after the children for me?'

'So what did you want to talk to me about?' Veronica asked as soon as she had Elena safely alone.

Elena stopped walking. They were halfway up the stone steps.

'Are you going to see Leonardo again?'

Veronica decided not to lie to Elena. 'Yes. Next weekend.'

Elena frowned. 'Here?'

'No. We'll meet up somewhere. Rome, possibly. Or Venice.'

'Are you in contact by phone?'

'He's going to ring me tonight.'

Elena frowned. 'Do you know where he went last night?'

'Yes. To a charity ball in Milan.'

'Do you know who he went with?'

Veronica stiffened. 'No. Who?'

'Lila Bianchi. She's an Italian model. Very beautiful. Very sexy.'

'He…he said he was going alone,' Veronica choked out.

Elena stared at her, then shook her head. 'I knew it. You *are* in love with him.'

'I…' Veronica closed her eyes against the dismay which flooded through her. She'd known all along what kind of man Leonardo was. But even she hadn't thought he would lie to her like that.

'Come,' Elena said, and took her arm. 'I will show you the photos. They are all over social media this morning.'

When they got up to the villa, Elena pulled her phone out of her pocket and brought up the photos of the ball. There were several of Leonardo with this Lila woman draped all over him. In one photo they were dancing cheek to cheek. In another, she was kissing his neck. The final straw, however, was the one of him going arm in arm with that creature into some apartment building.

Nausea swirled in Veronica's stomach, bile rising into her throat. She swallowed, then looked away. 'I don't want to see any more,' she said. 'I've seen enough.'

'I am ashamed of my brother,' Elena said forcefully. 'He is not worthy of you.'

'No,' Veronica agreed. 'He isn't.'

'Are you going to see him again?'

'No.'

'Please don't tell him I showed you the photos. He will be very angry with me.'

'I won't even mention that I have seen them. I'll make up some excuse and tell him that I'm going home ASAP.'

'Oh. Now I feel awful. I should not have told you. I have spoiled your holiday.'

Veronica's smile was sad. 'You did the right thing, Elena. And I thank you. Please don't worry. You've saved me from making an even bigger fool of myself.'

'Leonardo is the fool,' Elena snapped.

'He will be a lonely old man one day,' Veronica muttered, then came forward to give Elena a hug. 'He won't ever have what you and Carmelina have. Yes, you're right. He is a fool. Now, go back to your husband and children and be happy. I have to ring the airline and change my flight.'

After Elena left, Veronica slumped down on the terrace and tried to get her head around those awful photos, especially the last one she'd looked at. Impossible to pretend there was any logical explanation for them. They spoke for themselves. Leonardo had gone to the ball with that creature and no doubt taken her to bed afterwards.

This last realisation brought a wealth of pain. And a rush of tears.

How could Leonardo have lied to her like that? she agonised. What kind of man was he?

The kind of man you've always known he was, came the bitter answer.

A playboy and a player.

No way, Veronica determined as she dashed away the tears, was she going to give him the opportunity to lie to her again. And he would lie, if she confronted him with those photos when he rang her tonight. No... she intended to do what she'd said to Elena. Make up some excuse why she had to go home ASAP and then cut him dead.

CHAPTER TWENTY-EIGHT

LEONARDO HAD TO have a lie-down late that Sunday afternoon, something which he couldn't remember doing in years. Last night had been a nightmare, with Lila having latched onto him as soon as he'd arrived at the ball and made it impossible for him to extricate himself from her clutches without being rude. If she hadn't already been contracted as the main model for next season's ski-wear, he would have told her to get lost in no uncertain words.

Of course, she'd been totally stoned. On top of that, she'd had an argument with her boyfriend and come alone, determined to find some man to make the boyfriend jealous. Leonardo had been an excellent mark, since he was handsome, rich and, in a way, her boss. He'd been in a no-win situation from the start, unable to get rid of her, yet knowing full well that everything he did would be photographed and misinterpreted, fodder for all the gossip websites and magazines.

Never had a night seemed so long, or so emotionally exhausting. He'd had to smile and make speeches, all the while worrying what Veronica would think if she saw reports of him dancing with Lila at the ball. Not that she was likely to. Capri was rather isolated when it came to mainland gossip. Though there was always social media. Nowhere was safe any more. Best he tell her about it upfront tonight, even the part about having had to see the stupid girl safely home at some ungodly hour. She would understand. Surely? Veronica was quite the pragmatist. And not given to dramatising things.

A glance at his watch showed it was just after four in the afternoon. He'd promised to ring her this evening. When did evenings start, exactly? he wondered. Seven? Eight? He wanted to hear her voice. Wanted to hear her say, *yes, Leonardo, of course I'll spend next weekend with you. Wherever you like, darling.*

He doubted she would go that far. Just 'yes' would do for now.

Dio, he was tired. Yawning, Leonardo closed his eyes and drifted off.

Veronica couldn't get a flight until Wednesday, not on the same airline and without spending a small fortune by upgrading to business class. She supposed she could last until then. Her flight took off early in the morning, so she would make her way to Rome on the Tuesday then stay at one of the airport hotels that night.

She spent the rest of the afternoon keeping busy so that she didn't fall into a depression. She packed, cleaned the bathroom then returned to the living room to read another of her father's books. This time, it didn't hold her attention. In the end, she put it down and went out onto the terrace.

By the time her phone rang just after seven, she felt very down. But furious as well. When she saw Leonardo's name on her screen, she wanted to throw the damned phone against the wall. But she didn't. Her fingers tightened, as did her lips.

'Leonardo,' she said in a rather droll tone. 'You remembered to ring.'

His hesitation to answer showed he'd heard the sarcastic edge in her voice.

'But of course,' he replied at last. 'Did you doubt me?'

Doubt him?

No, she didn't doubt him. She'd known he would ring.

'I don't have a lot of faith in the opposite sex,' she said truthfully. 'But I'm very glad you rang,' she swept on. 'Unfortunately, my mother is not well and I have to go home earlier than expected, so I'm afraid I can't join you next weekend.'

Again, a few seconds went by before he spoke. 'What is wrong with her?' he demanded to know, as though sensing she was lying to him.

'She's always had a weak chest. When she gets a cold, it quickly becomes bronchitis, which sometimes turns into pneumonia.' Actually, this was quite true. But of course Nora didn't have a cold at the moment.

'She has pneumonia?'

'Not yet. But it's heading that way if she doesn't rest.'

'I see.'

'I'm sorry to disappoint you, Leonardo, but it's a case of family first. My flight leaves on Wednesday morning. Anyway, it's not as though we were going anywhere. It was just a fling, as you very well know.'

'No, I do not know,' he bit out. 'Maybe it was to begin with but I thought... I hoped...'

He actually sounded upset.

Too bad, Veronica thought angrily. The man was a

bastard. And a liar. The only thing he hoped for was more sex.

'I'm sorry,' she said with little apology in her voice, 'But I did warn you. Now, about the villa…'

'You want to talk *business* with me?' His astonishment was obvious.

'Why not? You still want the villa, don't you?'

'I don't feel like talking business with you right now,' he said coldly. 'I will contact you via email after you arrive home. Goodbye.' And he hung up.

Veronica blinked at the abruptness with which he'd ended the call, all her anger dissipating in the face of the reality that it was over. Never again would he kiss her. Never again would he hold her in his arms. Never again…

Before she could work out her emotions, she threw herself down on the lounge and wept long and hard.

CHAPTER TWENTY-NINE

It SEEMED TO take for ever for Tuesday to come. On the Monday Veronica bit the bullet and walked down to the Hotel Fabrizzi, repeating her lie about her mother's illness and saying her goodbyes, as well as quietly reassuring a worried Elena that she hadn't mentioned anything to Leonardo about the photos she'd shown her. All the Fabrizzis seemed genuinely sorry to see her go, which made Veronica feel even worse than she was already feeling.

Later that day she rang her mother and did her best to sound composed.

'I'm coming home even earlier than I said. My flight leaves Rome on Wednesday morning.'

'Oh, that's a shame. You really needed a long holiday.'

'Perhaps. But not here.'

'I see,' she said with a wealth of knowingness. 'Have you taken the second test yet?'

'No. I'll do it when I get home.' If by some awful twist of fate it was positive, she didn't want to be here when she found out.

'Right. Do you want me to meet you at the airport?'

'Heavens, no. That madhouse? I'll catch a taxi home.'

'Are you sure you're all right?' she asked, sounding worried.

'I'll survive, Mum. See you on Wednesday. Take care.' And she hung up before she could burst into tears again.

When Veronica finally came to pack the second pregnancy test, she stared at it for a long time. Then curiosity—or maybe it was masochism—got the better of her. So she carried it into the bathroom and did what she had to do.

Afterwards, she put the stick down on the vanity and walked out, unable to stand there waiting. Was it her imagination or were her breasts suddenly tingling? Surely fate couldn't be that cruel? She paced around the bedroom for the required time then charged back into the bathroom, snatching up the stick.

'Oh, no!' she cried when she saw the result. 'It can't be!'

But it was. It very definitely was. She was pregnant with Leonardo Fabrizzi's child.

Her stomach suddenly heaved and she only just bent over the toilet in time. After flushing away her dinner, she washed out her mouth and returned to the bedroom, where she collapsed on the bed. Her head continued to whirl and she could hardly think straight.

How could this have happened? she wailed to herself.

The usual way, you idiot, returned her pragmatic side. *You took a risk and now you're going to have to pay the price. Serves you right for relying on the rhythm method. What sensible girl does that these days? And what sensible girl sleeps with a playboy like Leonardo Fabrizzi without using condoms?*

'Oh, God… Leonardo,' she groaned aloud.

He was going to be even more upset than her when she told him. More than upset. He'd be furious with her for having lied to him about the pill. But she would have to tell him about the baby at some stage, because no way was a child of hers going to be brought up without knowing who its father was. Lord, no!

Perhaps she wouldn't tell him until she was safely past the three-month stage when the threat of miscarriage had passed.

Thinking about miscarrying her baby made Veronica realise that deep down she didn't want that to happen any more than she wanted to have a termination. This was her child growing inside her, a child born out of love. She could at least admit to herself that she loved Leonardo. Which was perverse, given the kind of man he was. But then life was perverse, wasn't it?

Her hands came to rest across her stomach as she contemplated what it would be like to be a mother. She hoped she would be a good one. Kind and caring, but not a helicopter mother. Her own mother hadn't been that, for which she was grateful. She'd allowed Veronica considerable freedom as she'd grown, encouraging her to work as well as to study, to become her own person. She knew she had considerable strength of character when needed. And she would need it now.

The next morning she had a good breakfast, after which she washed everything up—there wasn't enough to load a dishwasher—then finished off packing her one case. At eight-thirty she locked up and placed the key back in the geranium pot. Thankfully the weather was still good, if a little cloudy. She hadn't called a taxi, Franco having insisted that he would pick her up from the Hotel Fabrizzi to drive her down to the jetty. She stood for a long moment on the terrace, gazing out at the gorgeous view and putting it into her memory bank, though she suspected it might not be the last time she saw it. Leonardo would not let his child go easily. Neither would Sophia and Alberto. But she would not think about that yet. Time enough when she had a healthy ultrasound in her hands.

As she headed off towards the path, tears pricked at her eyes. She turned to have one last, longing look at her father's villa, wondering at the same time if he'd ever envisaged this happening when he'd made his will. Had he hoped that she and Leonardo would end up together? It seemed rather fanciful.

Dragging her case behind her, she started walking down the steep path, dashing away tears at the same time. It happened so quickly. She caught her heel in something and pitched forward. A scream of terror burst from her lips as she crashed down onto the uneven stone steps. Her head hit something and everything went black.

Veronica woke slowly to a dull headache and a strange bedroom, not to mention a strange man sitting on a chair beside the bed she was lying in. He was quite elderly with a neat white beard and white hair—though perhaps he was not as old as he looked, since his blue eyes were clear and his face not too wrinkled.

'Where am I?' she asked groggily. 'And who are you?'

'You're in a guest room at the Hotel Fabrizzi, and I'm Dr Waverly.'

She blinked at him. 'You're English.'

'Yes. I semi-retired to Capri many years ago but continued to practise for people who wanted an English-speaking doctor. I was Ruth's doctor until she died. And Laurence's, when he deigned to go to a doctor. Which wasn't often. Sophia called me in because she thought you would be best with an English doctor. So, how are you feeling, my dear?'

'Rotten.'

'I can imagine. You had a bad fall and you've been unconscious for over a day. Concussion. Would you mind if I examined you?'

Veronica blinked, struggling to remember the circumstances of this fall.

'What kind of examination?'

'Nothing too intrusive. I just want to check you over. Make sure you're on the road to recovery.'

'How long did you say I've been out of it?' she asked as he took her blood pressure.

'Just over twenty-four hours.'

'Oh, Lord!' she said, sitting up abruptly. 'I've missed my flight. I have to ring Mum and tell her.'

'Leonardo's already rung her and explained.'

Veronica gaped at him. 'Leonardo's talked to my mother?'

'It seems so. And he wants to talk to you. Shall I call him in? He's just outside.'

'No!' she cried out.

'He knows about the pregnancy, Veronica.'

She slumped back on the pillows, her head thumping. 'But how?' she choked out.

'You never stopped talking about it when you were

semi-conscious. You were worried that you might lose the baby.'

'Oh…'

'You haven't, by the way. Your baby's fine.'

Veronica closed her eyes, tears of relief leaking out. Being pregnant by Leonardo wasn't ideal, but she didn't want to miscarry.

'It is Leonardo's, isn't it?' the doctor asked gently.

She nodded wearily.

'Are you absolutely sure you're pregnant?'

'I did one of those tests. It was very positive.'

'No need for a blood test, then.'

'You can do one if you like.'

'Knowing Leonardo, perhaps it would be best.'

'Yes, I would imagine so,' she said, somewhat bitterly. 'Though he needn't worry about my trying to trap him into marriage. Because I wouldn't marry him, no matter what!'

The doctor made no comment, just got a syringe out of his bag and took a sample of her blood. 'You don't love him?' he asked after a while.

She refused to answer, her emotions a mess, anger and distress mingling with fear. Leonardo was here. And he'd talked to her mother! What had they talked about? What had Nora told him?

The doctor looked perplexed. 'I think I should tell Leonardo to come in.'

Before Veronica could protest, he stood up and carried his bag outside. Through the open door she could hear the murmuring of voices. And then there he was, standing in the doorway, looking as handsome as ever rather strained. There were dark shadows around which held an expression of real concern.

Or possibly she was mistaken about that. Maybe it was just controlled anger fuelling the tension in his face.

After a momentary hesitation, Leonardo came in, closed the door and sat down in the chair the doctor had vacated.

'Dr Waverly said you must rest easy for a few more days,' he said coolly. 'Your blood pressure is up.'

'I feel fine,' she returned stubbornly, and looked away from him.

A silence fell in the room, Veronica aware of the pulse beating in her temples.

'Were you ever going to tell me about the baby, Veronica?' he demanded to know. 'Or was I just to be a sperm donor, like Laurence?'

Outrage had her head whipping back to face him.

'Do you honestly think I would deliberately get pregnant by you? Or that I would choose to be a single mother? I know how hard that life is.'

He nodded. 'Yes, I can appreciate that. And, no, I don't think you *deliberately* set out to get pregnant. But you were never on the pill, were you?'

'Oh, God. Mum told you I wasn't, didn't she?'

'No. I was just guessing. Your mother did tell me about Jerome, however. I think she wanted to explain why you mistrusted my intentions so much, and why you would try to bolt home once you realised you were pregnant. Which, by the way, was news to your mother. She said you did a test and it was negative.'

'The first time it was,' she muttered. 'I did a second test later on and it was positive. If you don't believe me, ask Dr Waverly. He's taken a blood sample to double-check. I thought you might want proof,' she threw at him, her top lip curling with contempt.

'No,' he denied with amazing calm. 'Not really. I can see that you're not lying. But you did lie to me about being on the pill, didn't you?'

'Not at first,' she said with a frustrated sigh. 'You asked me if there was any danger of a pregnancy and I told you there wasn't. That was because I'm always very regular and I honestly thought there was no risk of conceiving that weekend. You just assumed I was on the pill and it seemed easier to let you think that.'

'So what went wrong?'

'I don't know!' she wailed, stuffing a fist against her trembling mouth and shaking her head. 'I guess finding out about my real father upset my cycle somehow. I could hardly believe it when I was late.'

'I see,' he said slowly. 'Don't you want my baby, Veronica?'

She opened her mouth to snap that of course she didn't. But then she shut it again. She could not keep lying to him. She just couldn't. So she didn't say anything.

'*I* want it,' he said softly into the silence. 'And I want you. I love you, Veronica.'

Her eyes grew wide with shock, and the most awful hope.

Oh, Veronica, don't fall for the 'I love you' ploy, she told herself sternly.

'You're just saying that because you want your child.'

'I am not in the habit of lying,' he returned. 'Which reminds me,' he continued before she could laugh in his face. 'Elena told me about the photos she showed you. Of me and Lila at the ball. I didn't lie to you, Veronica. I went to that ball alone. Lila threw herself at me as soon as I got there and it was impossible to extricate myself from her cling-on tactics without making a scene. I wouldn't have been so tolerant if she hadn't been hopelessly drunk and very upset over a fight with her boyfriend. She wasn't making a serious play for me, Veronica. We've known each other for years and there's nothing between us. She was just trying to make her boyfriend jealous. And it worked too. They're back together again. I was going to tell you all about it when I rang last Sunday night but you didn't give me the chance. If you don't believe me, I'll have her come down here personally so that she can explain her behaviour.'

Veronica stared at him for a long time without blinking. Could he be telling the truth? Maybe he did care for her. Maybe he even loved her. Just the hope of it sent her head into a whirlwind.

Leonardo leant over and took both her hands in his. 'I care deeply for you, Veronica. It took me a while to accept my feelings but they are real, I assure you. When I rang you last Sunday and you said what you said, in such a cold voice, I was devastated. Because I'd arrogantly thought you cared for me back.'

'I… I do care for you,' she said hesitantly. 'But…'

'But you think I'm a playboy who is incapable of commitment and true caring.'

'Yes…'

'I have been a bit of a bad boy in the past, I admit. But I haven't been all that bad for some years now. Yes, my girlfriends don't last long. Perhaps because I didn't fall in love with any of them. But I never cheated or treated them shoddily. If nothing else, I've always been a gentleman.' And, lifting her hands to his lips, he kissed every finger gently. Reverently. Lovingly.

Veronica's heart turned over.

His head lifted at last and he looked deep into her eyes. 'I love you, Veronica. More than I ever thought possible. Dare I hope you love me back?'

She could not speak, her heart too full. Tears flooded her eyes. It was all too good to be true. She found it almost impossible to believe.

His sigh was heavy. 'I see you still don't trust me. Understandable, considering what you went through with that other unconscionable bastard. But, if you just tell me that you love me, I will move heaven and earth to prove to you that I am a man of my word.'

'I… I do love you. But how…how do you propose to prove yourself?' she asked, moved by his passionate declaration.

'By not proposing marriage, for starters, even though that is my dearest wish—to have you as my wife. I have a lovely home in Milan where I think we could be very happy together. But I can see you are not ready to take that step yet. So this is what I propose instead. Your mother said I was welcome to stay at her home whenever I liked, so I will take her up on her offer. I can run my business over the Internet. I have excellent staff who are very capable. So I will come to Sydney and live there with you—without sex—until you can see first-hand and up close what kind of man I am. An honourable man who will make you a good husband and a very good father.'

'You would do that for me?' she choked out, overcome with emotion.

'I would do anything for you.'

'Oh!' she exclaimed, sitting up and throwing her arms around his neck.

He held her close, kissing her hair and telling her over and over how much he loved her.

Veronica could scarcely believe the wave of happiness that claimed her. She'd been so unhappy for so long. So cynical as well. But Leonardo had blasted that cynicism to pieces just now with his incredible offer. She wasn't too sure about the 'no sex' part, but if he could do it then so could she.

And so it was that just over three months later, on the evening after they went together to have their first ultrasound—the baby was healthy and a boy—Leonardo took Veronica out for dinner where he produced the most glorious ring and asked her to marry him.

Leonardo would remember the look on her face for ever. It was filled with a joy which came not just from love but absolute faith. It had taken time for her to totally trust him. Time and sacrifice on his part. He was not a man used to denying his male urges. But it had been worth it in the end.

'You were the right girl that Laurence talked about,' he said as he slipped the diamond ring on her finger. 'This was what he wanted when he made sure that we would meet.'

'That thought did occur to me once too,' she replied, surprising him.

He was very thankful now that he'd never told her what he'd found on Laurence's phone. He hadn't been sure that she would be pleased with her father researching the female biological clock the day before he'd gone to London and changed his will. He would not have liked Veronica to assume that her father was more concerned about her being childless than anything else. It was possible, he supposed, but Leonardo preferred to believe that his friend wanted his daughter and his friend to meet, fall in love and hopefully marry.

Whatever his motives, it had all worked out in the end.

I have found a new dream, Laurence. A better one. I am going to be the best husband and father in the whole of Italy. Maybe even in the whole world!

Hopefully, if Laurence were able to observe things from heaven—or wherever he was—he would approve.

As for Leonardo's own family, they would be over the moon now that marriage was on the horizon. His *mamma* was already making preparations for a big wedding on Capri. Nora had been in constant contact with her and the two women were happy little conspirators.

He smiled over at Veronica, who was touching her ring and looking very thoughtful.

'What is it?' he asked, very in tune with her feelings by now.

'I was just wondering…'

'Wondering what?'

'If I could spend tonight in the guest room. With the man I adore.'

Leonardo took a deep breath, letting it out slowly as emotion claimed him. He'd always thought that nothing would ever surpass winning a race on the ski slopes.

He was so wrong.

EPILOGUE

March the following year...

'YOU LOOK ABSOLUTELY BEAUTIFUL,' her mother said, her voice catching.

They were alone in the master bedroom of Laurence's villa, getting ready for what was going to be the wedding of the year on Capri. The official invitations numbered over three hundred, with guests coming from all over the world, their expenses paid for by Leonardo. The wedding was to take place in Santo Stephano, the main church on Capri, the reception at the Grand Hotel Quisisana, a five-star hotel which exuded both history and luxury.

Veronica didn't like to think of what the bill might be, Leonardo having brushed aside her worries with his usual *savoir faire*.

'I am not going to stint on our wedding, Veronica,' he'd said when she'd broached the subject. 'You deserve everything I can afford to give you.'

It seemed that what he could afford was one hell of a lot. Her wedding dress had been designed by one of the best designers in Milan, with Veronica not even having been told what it had cost. And the gown was, in truth, a breathtakingly lovely creation, designed to hide perfectly her six-and-a-half-month baby bump without compromising on elegance.

There was a floor-length under-dress made in white chiffon, which was princess-line in style and sleeveless, with a scooped neckline and softly gathered skirt. Over this lay a long, white lace coat that had long sleeves and flowed out the back in a train. There was only one button, just under her bust, though one could hardly call it a button. It was a jewelled clasp, made of pearls and diamonds, as were the drop earrings that Leonardo had given his bride as an additional wedding present. Her hair was up, a circlet of flowers crowning her dark tresses. Attached at the back was a simple tulle veil that had a small face veil which could be brought over her face then lifted during the ceremony.

Veronica looked at her mother and smiled. 'I do look good, don't I?'

'I think that's an understatement, my darling daughter. Laurence would be so proud.'

'I like to think so,' she said, still feeling a little sad when she thought of the missed opportunities with her father.

'Come, now. No sad thoughts today. You are on your way to be married to one of the nicest, most sincere men I have ever met. Not to mention the most generous. But first, we have to join the others and have photos taken on the terrace.'

The 'others' were considerable. Veronica had been unable to resist asking both Elena and Carmelina to be her matrons of honour, Leonardo going along with her by making Franco and Alfonso his best men. All their children were in the wedding party as well as flower girls and page boys. They were thrilled to pieces to be asked and promised to be very good, even the precocious Bruno having given his solemn word. The matrons of honour were in sky-blue silk and carried white bouquets, the flower girls in white with white-and-blue posies. All the men—and boys—had chosen to wear black tuxedos, all made in Milan, their lapels carrying white roses.

Nora—as mother of the bride—had chosen pale lemon, her elegantly styled suit also having been made by a top designer in Milan. She looked lovelier—and happier—than Veronica had ever seen her. Her mother was in the process of selling her home-help business and moving to Capri, where she would live in Laurence's villa, looking after it for Veronica and Leonardo for when they could come and stay. Which Veronica vowed would be often. The happy couple had already made their permanent home in Milan, the nursery all ready for their son's arrival. Francesca, Leonardo's housekeeper, was very excited at the thought of having a baby in the house. Luckily, she and Veronica liked each other, which had pleased Leonardo greatly.

Last in the wedding party was Dr Waverly, who'd agreed to give Veronica away. He'd seemed a good choice, being a friend of her real father, and of his vintage.

The photos took a good while, the sky being a little cloudy, though every now and then the sun would peep out. At least it wasn't raining. The weather on Capri in March could be very capricious. At last the photos were all finished to the photographer's satisfaction and it was time to head to the waiting cars, the bride having chosen to travel in Franco's yellow convertible, the rest in other equally colourful taxis. Just as Veronica made her way off the terrace, the sun came out again, bathing the villa in glorious light. Veronica glanced over her shoulder and thought how her father's home had never looked more beautiful.

Her father...

Yes, she hadn't known him in life, but she'd got to know him in death, lots of people having filled her in on his character. No, he hadn't been a perfect man, but he had been a good man, and a brilliant scientist who'd made a difference in the world through his work. He'd also been a man capable of great love. Veronica felt she had inherited that quality from him, because she loved Leonardo and their unborn baby more than she could ever have thought possible. She could not wait for her son to be born and to see what their genes would produce. A very special child, she was sure. Very special indeed.

But none of this would have happened, she thought as she gazed back at the villa, if her father hadn't left her his home in his will.

'Thank you, Dad,' she murmured, her heart filling with gratitude and love. 'Thank you.'

Their son was born in May, three weeks early, obviously impatient to come into this world. He was perfect in every way, captivating everyone who saw him. They called him Antonio Laurence Alberto Fabrizzi. His grandfather was thrilled. At last, a boy who would carry on his name. Antonio's two grandmothers were besotted, but not as much as his parents, who vowed to have more children as soon as possible.

* * * * *

#3669 SICILIAN'S BRIDE FOR A PRICE
Conveniently Wed!
by Tara Pammi
To counter a business threat, ruthless Dante must get married! Free-spirited Alisha will do anything to save her mother's charity—even marry Dante. But the price of their marriage is more than they bargained for...

#3670 HER FORGOTTEN LOVER'S HEIR
by Annie West
Pietro is stunned to learn Molly is pregnant—but an accident leaves Molly with no memory of him! Pietro must help Molly remember their fierce attraction, and the fact that the baby she's carrying is the Agosti heir...

#3671 REVENGE AT THE ALTAR
by Louise Fuller
Nothing gives Max more satisfaction than hearing Margot say "I do." Though he was rejected by her family once before, this time, Max holds all the cards! But their wedding night tempts Max to forget revenge...

#3672 A RING TO CLAIM HIS LEGACY
by Rachael Thomas
Marco can't forget the woman he spent a week with on a luxurious island. So when he learns she's expecting his baby, he's convinced their child will secure his family's dynasty...

_____

Get 4 FREE REWARDS!

We'll send you 2 FREE Books plus 2 FREE Mystery Gifts.

Harlequin Presents® books feature a sensational and sophisticated world of international romance where sinfully tempting heroes ignite passion.

FREE
Value Over
$20

*When shy Molly is found sobbing by Salvio, he comforts
her...with the most amazing experience of her life. But
when it costs Molly her job, she must become Salvio's
temporary housekeeper—just in time for Christmas!*

*Read on for a sneak preview of
Sharon Kendrick's next story,*
The Italian's Christmas Housekeeper.

"The only thing that will stop me is you," he continued,
his voice a deep silken purr. "So stop me, Molly. Turn
away and walk out right now and do us both a favor,
because something tells me this is a bad idea."

He was giving her the opportunity to leave but Molly
knew she wasn't going to take it—because when did
things like this ever happen to people like her? She
wasn't like most women her age. She'd never had sex.
Never come even close, despite her few forays onto a
dating website that had all ended in disaster. Yet now
a man she barely knew was proposing seduction and
suddenly she was up for it, and she didn't care if it was
bad. Hadn't she spent her whole life trying to be good?
And where had it gotten her?

Her heart was crashing against her rib cage as she stared up into his rugged features and greedily drank them in. "I don't care if it's a bad idea," she whispered. "Maybe I want it as much as you do."

Don't miss
The Italian's Christmas Housekeeper,
available November 2018 wherever
Harlequin Presents® *books and ebooks are sold.*

www.Harlequin.com